Cherished Blood

The Erotic Vampire Series
Blood Kiss
Erotica Vampirica
Cherished Blood

Cherished Blood
Sensual Vampire Stories

edited by Cecilia Tan

Circlet Press, Inc.
Cambridge, MA

Cherished Blood

Circlet Press, Inc.
1770 Massachusetts Avenue #278
Cambridge, MA 02140
http://www.circlet.com/circlet/home.html
circlet-info@circlet.com

Typeset in the United States of America
Printed in Canada
Text design and typesetting by Swordsmith Productions

ISBN 1-885865-18-X

First Printing: October 1997

Circlet Press is distributed in the USA and Canada by the LPC Group.
Circlet Press is distributed in the UK and Europe by Turnaround Ltd.
Circlet Press is distributed in Australia by Bulldog Books.

Retail, wholesale, and bulk discounts are available direct from Circlet, or from the fine wholesalers who carry our line of books, including Alamo Square Distributors, AK Distributors, Bookazine, Bookpeople, Koen Book Distributors, Last Gasp of San Francisco, and Pacific Pipeline. In the United Kingdom and Europe, Circlet Press is represented to the trade by Turnaround, Ltd., London.

Contents

Drink to Me Only with Thine Eyes—

A. R. Morlan

Not very long after making my way to the great, glittering night-jewel of a city known to simple mortals as New York, very soon after I opened my store in fact, I commissioned a fellow artisan to hand-ink a framed scroll which now hangs above the counter located toward the rear of my showroom:

> *"The Beginning of Wisdom is Learning to Call Things by Their Right Names."*
> **—An Ancient Chinese Saying**

Originally, I intended the sign merely to provide a gentle reminder to my customers about the importance of knowing the difference between soft and hard pottery, or of glazed ware from enamel ware . . . for while I am a master of long standing (the longest standing) in the ancient art of creating pottery of all forms and of virtually all historical styles, it still causes me pain to hear someone ask for a "porcelain flowerpot" or "something simple—like a Ming vase, maybe?" Yet, whenever my customers read the sign today, in this time of names more bizarre than any I have previously heard in my many centuries of wandering the ever-shifting, blood-scented starlit darkness—eccentric jumblings of the Anglo-Saxon and the African, Gaelic and Germanic, with scatterings of names purloined from my native Orient—they invariably take my words as an invitation to explain their own idiosyncratic appellations to me, even as they dismiss my own name (albeit a common one among my countrymen long before I ceased to be a member of the Chinese—or human—race) without comment.

And always, when they pause in their perusal of the examples of my art available for immediate sale, and glance up at the inked scroll, they begin their personal litany with some variation of this question:

"'Right names' . . . does that mean some names for things are wrong?"

"A name is considered wrong only as long as its true meaning remains unknown."

That's usually enough to set the customer off on his or her litany of why "my name is just right for me"—and, because (for the time being) that person *is* merely my customer, and not my impending evening's repast (*if* I can abide their continued presence), I fold my hands against my torso, widen the smile on my lips, and nod sagely as yet another potential meal explains the original meaning of his or her first or last name . . . or all three given names, if the customer is inexplicably proud of the *combined* meaning of his or her given title.

Personally, I choose to forget the meanings of names given to those customers I later rename "Sustenance" . . . and then, for the sole purpose of being able to tell any concerned relatives or friends who might drop by my establishment seeking information about their missing loved one that I never heard of such a person, especially by that name. . . .

But sometimes, I remember a name because the person bearing it holds the promise of being more than a nourishing interlude, a means to sate my unending, immortal hunger . . . and especially if that person is *not* so readily obtainable for my more personal needs.

Even if she had done no more than mention her name without elaboration, I would have been unable to forget it . . . or her; from the soft, petallike sheen of her flesh to the the subcutaneous throbbing of rich, heady blood in her veins and arteries to the guileless shimmer of her pale green-gold eyes, she was the epitome of feminine beauty and submerged passion. Far more beautiful in her unadorned simplicity than any of the wandering Empusae in ancient Greece, with their seductive, blood-sucking ways, or the Countess Bathory in all her blood-bathed glory . . . more desirable to me than any concubine from my native China, even in the sunlit days of my life, before the long-nailed nocturnal demon *Kian-si* favored me with a form of half-life after what should've been my certain death at her daggerlike hands.

Spurred on by the unspoken challenge of my sign, she not only uttered her name to me—"Trinette"—but then took pains to explain: "It's French, and means 'little innocent'—my mother, she was really into French culture and all, because she'd taken French in college, but we're really from Northern Italy, the blond part. I think it's a kind of . . . dumb name, but my boyfriend, he thinks it's cool. Of course, with him having a name like 'Cronan,' I suppose anything else *would* sound cool—"

How old can she be? I found myself wondering, even though the question was, of course, made moot by my own advanced sum of years; to me, the most wizened crone still able to draw breath was but a babe when I was celebrating my own several-thousandth (counting them can be far too depressing!) birthday by imbibing the lifeblood of what may well have been that wrinkled hulk's great-grandparent. . . .

Still, the obvious youth and inexperience of this maiden enchanted me, even as it intimidated me—I would, paradoxically, need to be less subtle, less suave than usual, in my pursuit or her, lest she simply not understand my import. Yet, I could not openly take her, steal her away to be my wife, for she was obviously promised to another—the scintillating small stone set in the ring on her left hand was a longstanding sign of her potential enslavement to another . . . this "Cronan" she spoke of so nonchalantly. . . .

"But surely, a name like 'Cronan' must have a right meaning of its own, no? A special meaning, like your name?" (I cringed at my own poor syntax, but to capture, sometimes one must provide suitable camouflage for the trap.)

Trinette smiled at my question, and said as she leaned against the counter which ran between us like a fireproof curtain protecting the fragile parchment from the hungering flame, "It's funny, but his name really does sorta describe him. . . . It means 'little dark one' in Irish, which he is on his mom's side, and it also means 'brown one' in Gaelic, which is what they speak in Scotland, where his dad's from. Like, literally. He was born there."

Moving her thin, delicate arms in a supple pushing motion which made her gently mounded breasts heave and fall under the restraining protective embrace of her blouse, she gracefully backed away from the counter. As she began strolling the widely-spaced aisles of low, glass-topped shelves upon which rested examples of my kiln-fired work, she added, "And that's where he and I will be moving once Cronan gets his degree. . . . He's studying medicine, only not to be a doctor, y'know, like a doctor-doctor, who treats sick people. Cronan's going to be a psychologist—"

As my would-be bride of blood prattled on and on about her earthly love, I watched the graceful, winglike swoop and flutter of her tapered fingers as they moved to almost-caress the surface of a lusterware pseudo-Greek vase, then hovered longingly before a translucent Sèvres plate, before actually descending to shyly touch the surface of a Sung-period (or celadone to people of her time and place) objet d'art—a small goblet, whose soft green gaze shone with a moist-fleshlike sheen in the store's indirect white lighting. . . .

(The image of our night of consummation was so clear to me, the details as sharply defined as one's reflection in porcelain:

(Trinette's bare arm moved languidly down my naked torso, the soft tender skin of her inner forearm brushing my own flesh, as her fingers walked down across my belly, toward my waiting organs of delight. And as gently as one might lift a paper-thin china tea cup, she slipped her hand, palm up, under my low-drooping globes of *yang* essence, then—with one coyly rubbing finger—she stroked the underside of my Jade Stalk, until it slowly stiffened in response to her tender ministrations.

(As my Jade Stalk rose, erect and as firm as the spout of a ceremonial teapot, my Trinette shifted beside me, revealing the long sloping curve of her bare back and globular buttocks as she moved herself into position over my triumphant organ. Carmine-daubed lips parted like two carved arcs of the finest cinnabar, then bent down her head of fiery-bright hair until the ends of her tresses brushed against my tensing thighs. And when her face was close to me, I could feel the soft exhalations of warm air against my throbbing stalk, just before a tongue-tip of exquisite, probing softness began to explore the glans and underside of my Vigorous Peak . . . followed by the sharp-edged glancing contact with her ivory incisors, which made my entire body tremble.

(Then my entire Jade Stalk, from tip to base, was engulfed in a cave of liquid, undulating warmth, caressed with a tongue which whipped from side to side like the lashings of a flicking cat's tail—and soon I felt the rushing warmth of yang essence flowing upward through my trembling manhood. But to squander my essence on a mere act of fellation would be wasteful, according to the old Masters of my race. Yang essence was limited in supply, especially for a being like myself, yet . . . this was my wedding night, to my precious bride of blood, so perhaps a *small* wasting of yang essence would be in order—

(Especially when my beloved's lips and tongue were so indescribably soft, and yet so urgent, in their ministrations. And so I did not go through the prescribed motions, of closing my eyes—for to do so would have deprived me of the sight of my beautiful one—pressing my tongue against the roof of my mouth, bending my back and stretching my neck, prior to opening my nostrils wide and closing my mouth, then sucking in my breath, in order to pull the semen back into my body. I did none of these long-prescribed things . . . but the reward of seeing my Trinette's face bent low over my groin, eyes closed in ecstasy as my yang essence rushed into her mouth, creating a kilnlike inferno around my throbbing Jade Stalk, was far greater than the conservation of my limited yang essence. . . .)

Turning her head quickly, so that her shoulder-length russet-brown hair moved, pendulumlike, in a sheaf of herbal-scented beauty, she asked, "Is this jade?"

Considering that there was now a good fifteen feet of floor space between us, I deemed it to be the most proper time to step out from behind my shieldlike counter and slowly, courteously, make my way toward her. Even from the chaste distance of five feet away, once I finally stood in place to speak to her, I could literally feel the throb of her lifeblood, calling to me in a deep, moist susurration that echoed in my very body. Calling upon my centuries-old reserve of willpower, I forced myself to smile once more, before replying, "No, it is merely a glaze upon the porcelain . . . but you are quite right in your supposition. Many people have mistaken Sung porcelain for carved jade."

(Or in your case, a Jade Stalk, I thought, as ripples of pleasure from my fantasy of her continued to course through my body.)

"Oh, that's a relief. . . . I didn't want you thinking I was dumb." Trinette smiled before moving down the aisle until she came to another, similarly-shaped drinking vessel I'd crafted. She cupped it as tenderly as a concubine cradling a man's Jade Stalk in her pink-suffused palm, and asked, "So I suppose this one is also pottery and not real jade?"

It had been over eighteen hundred years since I'd fired that particular drinking cup, back in the time of the Imperial kilns made available for the use of master potters like myself, yet the silky-smooth green glaze still shone as brightly . . . but only a total innocent like my Trinette (how those syllables rolled so vibrantly in my brain!) would confuse a piece of Han period pottery, with its simple, sturdy silhouette, with the supple, graceful curves of Sung period pottery.

But that ignorance suddenly made me aware of other, more useful gaps which she might have in her knowledge of my craft—not to mention in her knowledge of the center of my existence.

"What do you suppose is the difference between this bowl"—I cupped my hand under a small, glazed-ware piece I'd done as a time-killer while waiting for some Raku to cure—"and this bowl?" I finished asking, as I lifted up a granite-ware ashtray with the other hand. Trinette's liquid-fire eyes darted from one grayish glazed piece to the other, as her delectable mouth formed a small, coral-painted moue . . . then the darting flames of color in her dancing eyes grew warmer, as she replied confidently, "The price!"

The sly girl had peeked under each piece, so as to see the price sticker I'd affixed to the underside of their bottoms—and in doing so, had completely missed the crucial difference between the earthenware bowl, with its relatively plastic clay (which in itself was quite, quite close to soft pottery, save for the addition of a glaze), and the stoneware ashtray, with the greater percentage of strengthening silica in the clay mix—a percentage which ensured that the resulting piece, when fired, would be of close, hard inner texture.

Not an easy distinction to see, but it was a difference as crucial as trying to suck lifeblood from a painted, carved statue of marble, rather than the sleep-stilled neck of a cosmetics-adorned harlot. . . .

True, the upper surface of the bowl was quite similar to the utilitarian ashtray; both pieces were hard, shiny, mottled in color—but the unglazed undersides were

obviously unique to each piece, as individual as the
varying, sloping curves of a waiting neck. The bottom of
the bowl was akin to the flat end of a common flower pot,
while the other object's unseen surface was light and
flecked with infinitesimal spots of shining silica, much
like the small bright glints of light in the eyes of the
freshly-bitten. . . .

Warmed by the sanguine self-assurance which suffused
through my own rather tepid veins upon this latest
revelation of her blissful ignorance of my artistic domain,
I bade her to follow me down another aisle, to a low shelf
covered with naif-design flower pots designed to appeal to
Midwestern tourists and students low on funds. Then—
after selecting one of the pots—I gestured for her to follow
me up an adjoining aisle, where I'd arranged several of my
finest alkaline-glazed Chinese and Japanese-styled
teacups, each crafted of clay well-blended with silica and
kaolin . . . cups which were exceptional examples of
porcelain's resonance and infusibility, their upper rims
semitransparent, yet almost diamond-hard.

Gingerly picking up one of the palm-sized cups, I held
the pot and the cup before Trinette—

(even as I longed to hold my hands under the cuplike
softness of her gently swaying, unfettered breasts, my
thumbs lightly teasing her nipples into budding hardness,
before nuzzling her bared neck with my probing, pursing
lips, and aching, porcelain-tempered fangs. . . .)

—and asked in my most solemn, stereotypically Chinese-
merchant, butter-up-the-customer voice, "Touch each of
these, and tell me, what is the the difference between them?"
while I envisioned her touching parts of my own body, both
the soft and the hard. . . .

(Gratefully swallowing down my yang essence with a
tender smile, Trinette fondled my gradually-drooping Jade
Stalk with one hand, while running the other hand back

up my torso, until her fingers rested just below my jawline. Cupping my chin in her palm, she used her thumb to gently move my upper lip away from my incisors, then bent low to kiss me, her mouth still salty-sweet from my essence, her tongue prying itself between my teeth before mine slid forward to meet hers, in a pliant moist embrace—)

Suppressing a giggle, Trinette lightly caressed the unglazed, near-porous surface of the flowerpot, whose exterior might easily have been grazed by the jutting stone in her ring, then ran the same tapered finger over the superbly-glazed skin of the teacup, then shrugged, since I'd made sure that the bottoms, with their price stickers, were angled away from her clever green eyes.

"You can't even guess?"

She shrugged again, creating delicious folds of creamy flesh which briefly rose up to cradle the bottom of her neck, before she relaxed her shoulders.

Tilting the bowl and the pot so that she could see into them, I replied, in my best Chinaman-make-joke accent, "No hole in bottom!"

Her laughter was like glass wind chimes which formed a silvery descant to the throaty warble of the nightingale back in the land of my lost humanity, and I almost shed a tear at the memory of my former warmth and easily-rising passion and then limitless yang essence. But the reality of my current fate, and my unending need for both sustenance and (occasionally) emotional nurturing, kept the smile on my lips, and the twinkle in my eyes.

"That's a good one. . . . I'll have to remember it for Cronan. . . . Speaking of him, that's why I came in here—do you sell wedding goblets?" she asked, confirming the rightness of the plan I'd already begun to form for trapping—and keeping—her as my own.

"I do sell them . . . but first, I have to make them special, for each couple who request them," I replied, consciously slipping into the near-Pidgin dialect which seemed to put her more and more at ease with me, perhaps because it contrasted so well with the erudition of her someday-psychologist fiancé.

"Personalized?" she chirped, and my heart fluttered in time with her warbling voice. "Like with names and dates?"

"With anything they desire . . . any color, and any size goblet. For big thirst, or little thirst—"

"You'll have to make them plenty big. . . . Northern Italians and Scots-Irishman do love their wine." She smiled, and as her lips parted to reveal even, off-white teeth whose surfaces glinted in the store's white light, I imagined them bathed in the wine-red richness of my own immortal blood . . . blood which, when sipped by a mortal, had an effect which far surpassed intoxication, both in duration and in the resulting fire in the blood—

(And as our mouths pressed close in a firm-lipped embrace, Trinette began to writhe against me, her body burning from within as my ageless essence invaded each limb, each digit, with each hard-thudding beat of her heart, until all of her was infused with the most essential part of my being—my wedding gift of eternal life, of a hunger beyond mere physical sating, for my body, my essence. And only in the presence of one who'd partaken of my blood could my blood pulse strongly through my body, my Jade Stalk . . . my only possibility of true consummation was copulation with one of my own kind. . . .)

Even if I could not yet taste her blood, by the time she was lawfully wedded to her beloved Cronan, with the first sip from her special goblet, she would instead be mine and mine alone.

"Do you want your names and the date of the wedding on them?" I asked, suddenly all business (it was either that, or begin to chortle and dance around the aisles from the sheer exhilaration over what would occur during her wedding feast . . . an even I could literally picture in my mind's inner eye, it was so real and so vivid for me.)

"Yeah, but something else, too. . . . Wait a sec, I have it written down—" Trinette began to unzip her fanny pack, then rooted around in the bright green nylon pouch for something, until she gave me another radiant smile, and held up a sheet of paper covered with a couple of neatly handwritten lines, in an obviously masculine, but refined hand:

"*Drink to me only with thine Eyes,*
And I will pledge with mine"

I couldn't stop myself from smiling as I read those words; I'd been fortunate enough to hear Ben Jonson himself sing them, not long after he'd penned them in England so many, many years ago, and I felt a stab of longing for those gilded, passionate, yet elegant days, even as I felt an unexpected bond of . . . kinship for the man who'd selected the words for his as-yet uncrafted wedding goblets. Trinette's Cronan had to be quite a fine catch, especially for a young woman of her dubious intellectual gifts (bloodlust or no, I did realize that despite her physical charms, she was not . . . the sharpest incisor in the mouth).

"—wants them written or carved or whatever along the rim of the goblet, with the first line on his goblet, and the second one on mine," she was saying, as I forced myself to appear focused on her. "And could you make them red, or maybe even dark red? My bridesmaids will be in red velvet, only the maid of honor's going to be in *dark* red—"

Dark red indeed, I told myself, wistfully remembering the Cinnabar Clefts of my long-gone concubine conquests, as she went on and on about the size and shape of the goblets she had in mind. Oh, I will give you goblets—or rather, a goblet, my sweet innocent, my untasted wine—of a true, deep *blood* red. . . .

Trinette's wedding was to be in one month, more than enough time to prepare the special mixture of the most plastic, easily molded clay I could buy, plus an entire cup's worth (drained slowly, a few drips at a time, and always between my living feasts) of my own blood, and form the goblet by hand, partly by fast-kicked wheel, until it was ready for a glaze composed (again) mostly of my own eldritch blood, mixed with the more traditional glazing compounds. And just before I applied the living deep red glaze, I carefully incised the phrase

And I will pledge with mine

to that convex outer surface, forever marking the goblet as the one intended for my bride of deepest-red delights, that bearer of her own Cinnabar Cleft, a place my own lips would soon caress, even if the days of my last such nether-lipped were as distant as the last period of my own Jade Stalk's porcelain hardness, yet another tantalizing memory, albeit a soon-to-be-revived memory—

(Once Trinette's lips touch the wine-filled goblet, the flush begins with her lips, turning them a bloody-dark crimson, far darker than any modern lipstick, then progresses through her body, limb by limb, until she is covered with a blush of submerged fire . . . and it is with that warmth, radiating for her entire body pressed tightly against mine, that my long-dormant Jade Stalk rises once again, filled with a matching inner flame, the strength of blood seeking like-blood. . . .)

—white for Cronan's goblet, I used my finest siliceous clay, and merely the regular glaze. But once I'd fired the goblets, they looked remarkably similar, save for the differing lines of "The Forest: To Celia" that embellished their outer surfaces.

But even after they'd cooled, the goblet which was to caress the lips of my beloved-from-far-away was not quite ready. Inside the concave surface of the goblet, deep within the shadowed recesses of the breast-cupped interior, I used an iron nail to scratch off much of the glaze, so that the slightly porous inner clay was revealed. In turn it would release the essence of my blood, of my . . . uniqueness, into the acidic wine which would soon fill the goblet. Be it red wine or white, the acids in the potent brew would work a form of magic for me, distant, subtle legerdemain of the most insidious, infectious—yet sensuous—sort.

When Trinette's soft lips touched the goblet, and the sweet liquid-and-blood touched her waiting tongue, she would truly be a bride, of the most unholy sort. It was all I could do not to laugh aloud when she arrived to pick up the finished goblets, with her Cronan in tow, for even though he was a most comely young man, fine of limb and manly-fair of face (with his own hidden rushing spring of crimson fire under his fine-pored flesh), he would be no match at all for my plain-faced allure. . . .

On the night of their wedding feast, I paced the confines of my pottery studio located in back of my shop in anticipation of the coming of my longed-for blood-bride. True, she was not the first of my ensanguined mistresses of the night, but even for those of my kind, forever can become too, too much to contemplate, and so I'd been "widowed" many times, when those whom I'd converted through the sharing of my essence decided to in turn convert others more comely, or more to their liking, to the life of moon-kissed darkness and even darker desires and needs. But Trinette, my little innocent one, she longed for the kind of wisdom I possessed, the kind of power which comes with centuries of un-life, and the memories of countless nights of submerged passions—for didn't she breathe more deeply when speaking of her loved-one's love of education, of prestige?

For her, I could provide the erudition and status she longed for, plus the promise of life (or a dark-lusting simulation of it) eternal . . . all in exchange for perhaps a century or two of undivided adoration. . . .

Glancing at the ornate Swiss clock on the wall of my studio, I noticed that it was well past the time of the reception. It was being held only a few long blocks from my store, a miniscule walk or anxious run away. I began shivering with anticipation as sensual as any fleshly orgasm I'd once experienced, for I knew that the elixir of my eternity-tainted blood and her wine would prove irresistible to her, and would lure her on just as surely as the curved hook guides the silvery carp through the still, still waters, or the scent of the Open Peony Blossom attracts the ever-seeking upright Red Bird to a sheltering warm home—

The dry, frantic scraping of nails against my studio's alley door was echoed with the soft humming of "Greensleeves" behind that closed wooden barrier, the melody sinuous and melancholy in the night silence . . . and as I opened the door, I reflexively pulled back my lips and bared my porcelain-shiny incisors, in anticipation of sinking them (much like my own Red Bird, from my days of truly living flesh) deep into the bared bosom (in lieu of the Open Peony Blossom) of my blood-mate—

—who in turn was staring at me, eyes bright with
bloodlust and eager for that dark consummation of the
night . . . only they were eyes of warm amber-brown,
under waving short hair of deepest mahogany.

But before I could utter a single word of dismay, Cronan
smiled, his lips barely covering the already-growing incisors
lightly rimmed with blood-wine, and pantomimed an arms-
crossing gesture with his goblet-bearing hand . . . a motion
which had brought to *his* lips that goblet formed from clay
and blood, and glazed with a coating of my own inner
essence, fire-hardened into a glaze of near-diamondlike
vitrification. . . .

But yet, when he smiled, his eyes took on a warm, ale-
bright glow, one which was even more beautiful than the
green-gold fire of . . . of his newly jilted bride's eyes. And
as my wine-distilled blood raced through his fine features,
and suffused his flesh with a ruddy bloom, I nodded my
head in agreement with the wisdom—and rightness—of
his name, be it the Irish or the Gaelic interpretation, as I
moved my working fingers down his shirt, revealing his
well-muscled, darkly-tufted chest button by undone
button—and when my hand reached his waistband, he
placed both of his warm hands on mine, and fervently
nodded his assent as I unbuttoned and unzipped his
tuxedo trousers, and let them fall down past his already-
erect Jade Stalk with a billowing *shuuush* of black fabric.

And, as my fingers gently eased his Jade Stalk out of his
briefs, before massaging it from the base to the throbbing,
clear-pearl-adorned tip, Cronan's eyes fluttered closed,
even as his mouth gently parted, revealing the growing
buds of the ever-lengthening incisors within, while his
own seeking hands caressed my bared shoulders, and slid
palms-out along my jawline, in a motion so, *so* close to
my imagined wedding night with . . . with *her*.

And, as his own fiery yang essence warmed me from within, surging past my aching lips, I realized that once I referred to Cronan as my blood-mate, rather than blood-bride, a most wise choice had been made for me by fate.

For once Cronan knelt before me, and partook of my yang essence, there was no difference at all between the fantasy of a month ago and the reality of this night.

After all, as my sign in the shop says, it's all a matter of calling things by their right name. . . .

Just as a mate might be that of the soul, as well as the body. . . .

Blood Dreams

Susan Elizabeth Gray

The vampire's wife rolled toward the center of her bed. The sheets were cold and her husband's place was empty. She opened one eye and looked at the glowing red numbers of the digital clock. Two-thirty-one. Sunrise wasn't until six-twenty, so it would be at least another two hours until he came home, if not longer.

Theresa stretched, sliding her body over the satin surface of the sheets. She reached under her husband's pillow. The cloth bag of dirt was there, tied with a velvet ribbon. That was just one of many little idiosyncrasies that Theresa had to get used to since they'd met, at last year's Halloween party. Blake was dressed, of course, like Count Dracula. Underneath his cape he wore a white tie and tails, and he even had an ebony walking stick to complete the ensemble. Theresa had been persuaded to go to the party at the last minute, and all she could come up with was a pair of cat ears and a silky black dress. She drew whiskers across her cheeks and practiced a faint meow.

At the party, Theresa stood by the punch bowl, watching the friendly conversation and flirting swirl around her like confetti. Suddenly she became aware of someone standing beside her. He stood as silently as she, watching. Finally, he said, "If I had known the party was going to be this much fun, I would have come earlier."

Theresa laughed before she could stop herself and turned to see if she knew him. His hair was as black as his cape, and swept straight back off his forehead. He was so tall Theresa had to tip her head back to look at him. He smiled, clicked his heels together once and said, "Count Dracula, at your service. Or, you can call me Blake."

Theresa made a mock curtsy. "Theresa," she meowed.

"A pleasure," he said, as he took her hand. He raised it to his lips and Theresa shivered at their cool touch.

They spent the rest of the evening in a corner of the room, talking, and Theresa was impressed by his self-assurance and calm. He seemed to look at the world as she did, a few steps back, apart from the meaningless day-to-day trivia that consumed most of her friends.

He explained that he worked the night shift, but promised to call her on his break the next evening. When she left the party, he raised her hand again to his lips, but this time turned her palm upward and pressed it against his cheek. "You are so warm," he said.

DEAR DIARY: I met someone last night, finally. At the costume party. His name is Blake. I'm afraid to like him too much. I gave him my phone number. I hope he calls.

Three-ten. Theresa pulled the covers around her and turned to one side. She remembered how, at first, she didn't believe him. "You're just teasing," she said. It was only when he pulled her over to the mirror and stood right beside her that she began to believe, to feel the sharp edges of reality blur and soften. She turned to him, breathless, faint with the first stirrings of both fear and desire. She pressed her hand against his chest.

"How?" she asked.

He took her hand and led her over to the couch. Speaking slowly, in a quiet, measured tone as if talking to a child, he explained—explained how he had been born again so many years ago. Born of a woman, yes, but not his mother. How his appetite changed and how he must feed it every night. He tried, he said, to only take from those who wouldn't be hurt, those who were sick and dying anyway.

"But I thought vampires were evil," she whispered.

Blake looked down at her with glittering eyes. "We are," he said softly, and kissed her.

DEAR DIARY: Am I crazy?

The first time they made love, Theresa wept. He was so gentle, his hands so cool against her heated flesh. When she was ready, he paused, leaning above her. "I need to use protection," he said softly.

"No," she answered. "It's all right. I can't. Get pregnant."

"It's not that," he said, and slid to the side of the bed. He reached over and removed a small, foil package from the pocket of his pants. The condom crinkled as he unrolled it, smoothing it over his dark, erect penis.

He bent down and kissed her on the forehead. "You'll be safe," he said and entered her.

Afterward, when they had each been broken on the back of the wild horse, Theresa watched as he removed the condom, its tip full of blood.

DEAR DIARY: He asked me to marry him. I know what he is. But I have never met a man who is so gentle, so careful. He promised he would love me forever. I'm afraid of what that means.

They married at City Hall on a cold winter evening when the sun set shortly before five. No one was invited. The justice of the peace kept glancing at his watch, as if eager to get home to his well-lit house for dinner, a house filled with warm-blooded children and a plump wife. After the ceremony, they went to Theresa's favorite Italian restaurant. Blake, ever courteous, ordered pasta with marinara sauce, and claimed to be too full from a late lunch to finish his meal.

At the table, the wine glowing in the candle light like liquid rubies, Blake looked into Theresa's eyes and said, "I will never hurt you." She was surprised at the small sigh of disappointment rising in her breast.

DEAR DIARY: I cut my finger last night. It was eight o'clock and I was slicing vegetables for a stir fry. Blake is polite and lets me eat first, before he leaves to find his dinner, or should I say dinner partners? The knife slipped and sliced into the pad of my index finger. A bead of blood, garnet red. I could feel him stiffen and draw back, and his nostrils flared like a mad horse about to bolt. I don't know what came over me. I crossed the kitchen to where Blake was sitting at the round, oak table. The blood was still a bubble, thick and round at the tip of my finger. My heart was beating so hard I could barely breathe. I showed him and said, "Do you want to lick it?" He shook his head but I could see the desire rising in his eyes like mercury in a thermometer on a blistering hot July day. I took his hand and turned it, palm up, and placed it on the table. Then, with a boldness I didn't know I had, I squeezed the drop of blood from my finger until it lay, a small, red pool, in the center of his palm. I turned, and went back to the kitchen counter, to my slicing. The sucking sound behind me made chills run up and down my spine.

Theresa stirred again, and turned toward the clock. Four-seventeen. Not long now. She lowered her hand and pushed up the hem of her thin, silk nightgown. Her sex was warm and wet, waiting. Once, they had tried to make love before Blake went out for his evening meal. His body was cold and his penis felt like a core of ice entering her, sending icicles of pain flashing through her body. She pulled him closer, but no matter how tight she held him, he was still cold. And the way he looked down at her, with eyes as flat and black as wafers, black and empty. . . .

"You're so warm," he whispered. "Warm and full," he said, tracing one finger along the side of her throat. Then he pulled back, leaving her breathless.

Now they waited until he was full, his skin warm and rosy from the hot blood of others.

"Do you ever kiss them?" she once asked.

"Not on the lips," he replied.

DEAR DIARY: I hear the flutter of wings while I sleep. I think it's the others, come to brush against my windows, trying to get in. He told me his friends didn't understand how he could be married to a mortal, how they didn't think it possible to lie down each night next to a heart pumping fresh blood through veins and arteries, to be that close to living flesh and not take just one, luscious, mouthful of blood. Blake has told me the rules, though. They can't come in unless I invite them, but I'm still afraid. The sound is soft, like thick feathers brushing against the glass. Sometimes I hear my name. Sometimes I hear them laugh. I wish he could stay home to protect me.

Four-fifty-three. Theresa pushed back the covers and stretched her arms over her head. She hated waiting, never knowing if he'd had an easy evening and would come home early. Or whether he'd be in at the last minute, with barely enough time to undress and slide into bed before the sunrise. She swung her feet to the floor. The bedroom opened onto a balcony and Theresa crossed to the door to pull open the curtains. She pressed her fingers against the glass.

"Come home," she whispered to the night.

DEAR DIARY: I have to leave the house now, when I have my period. Blake said he would go, those few days each month when my body is ruled by the crimson tides of the moon. But the risk is too great, the risk that someone will find him as he sleeps during the day—find him and rouse the sleeping monster to full force. "It's a myth that sunlight melts us," he told me. "It just makes us mad and we have to strike back." So it's me that has to go.

Theresa opened the door to the balcony. The air was cool and she felt her nipples harden against the silk fabric of her nightgown. The moon was like a bowl of milk in the dark sky, and the light poured into the room. She shivered and hugged her arms around her waist. The sound of fallen leaves scuttling across the dry grass made her shudder. It was as if they, too, came alive at night to scratch at your legs.

She closed the door, but left the drapes open. She stepped across to the oval mirror which hung above the dresser. Theresa's hair glowed in the pale moonlight like a red star. She lifted her comb and started to pull it through the waves of her thick hair.

Without turning, she knew that Blake was suddenly behind her; she could feel the warmth rise from his body and smell the coppery scent of his breath. Theresa put down the comb and turned to face her husband.

"I was hoping you'd be home early," she said. Blake kissed her on the forehead.

"Let me wash up first," he said.

Theresa sat on the edge of the bed, listening to the sound of water running in the bathroom sink. She had wondered once, out loud, what would become of a vampire who lost his teeth. Blake stared at her. "We have other ways," he slowly answered.

The sound of the water stopped. Blake came into the room, his shirt already off. He sat down next to her on the bed. Theresa ran her fingers lightly over his bare chest, smooth and hairless, as unlined as that of a teenage boy. She pressed her palm flat against him.

"It's so strong," she said, feeling his heart beat underneath her fingers. "Are you full?" she said.

He nodded and drew her face close to his. "Kiss me," he said.

Theresa pressed her lips against Blake's warm mouth. She could feel the sharp edges of his incisors underneath his lips. Blake pushed gently on her shoulders until she was lying back against the pillows. With one hand, he reached for the waistband of his pants and unclasped his belt buckle. Theresa heard the urgent release of his zipper and moaned at the touch of his penis as it brushed against her leg.

She slipped off her nightgown as Blake reached into the nightstand drawer for a condom. Already, a red dot of moisture had formed on the tip of his penis. Before he could stop her, Theresa took one finger and smeared the blood on her fingertip. She raised her finger to his mouth and placed it between his lips. "Waste not, want not," she said, as he sucked.

Theresa watched as Blake unrolled the condom slowly over his penis. "Do you want me?" he whispered. Theresa reached for his penis. "Yes," she answered and moved her legs apart.

The darkness in the room was softening to gray around the edges, and Blake looked like a shadow as he rose over her and slid into her moist center. Theresa groaned and moved her hips to quicken his rhythm, but Blake stopped. "No," he said. "Not yet."

She looked up into his face. Blake's eyes were stars flickering against the velvet sky of their bedroom. Theresa felt a jolt as the light from his eyes penetrated hers and traveled down her spine. It felt like every nerve in her body had caught fire and small flames were licking her skin.

Theresa pressed against him, her arms clasped around his neck, her legs circling his back. She felt the thin membrane of flesh which separated them start to melt and she was unable to tell where she began and Blake ended. It was as if Blake was both inside and outside of her. She felt him surround her and for a single moment, no longer than the space between the beats of her heart, Theresa could not remember her name.

DEAR DIARY: I can't bear the thought of growing old next to him. I'm still young, but already I can see the lines forming around my eyes, across my forehead. He'll look the same, always. And he'll live without me, forever. I don't know if I can stand the thought of him being with another woman, even after I'm dead. I'm afraid to ask how many other wives he's had. The most he's told me is that he has never married

another vampire. Maybe the thought of eternity with the
same woman is too much for him.

Dawn was pressing against the edges of the dark window-
panes. It was almost time. Theresa went to the bathroom
to wash. Blake's shirt was on the floor, the collar flecked
with blood. She picked it up and held it to her face. It had
a strong smell—sweat, mixed with fear, laced with a sweet
perfume Theresa didn't recognize. She slid the shirt over
her naked torso and looked in the mirror.

"Could I do it?" she whispered to her reflection.
Theresa bared her teeth and ran her finger over the
sharpest one. She bit down, hard, and the metallic taste of
her own blood flowed into her mouth. She sucked, like a
child who has pricked her finger on a pin. Suddenly she
felt Blake rise up behind her.

"What are you doing?" he said.

Theresa remained silent.

He placed one hand on each of her shoulders and looked
down at her. "Do you want me?" he said. Blake's eyes
flashed, like a cat in the dark. Without blinking, he took
her hand and placed it on his throat.

"Feel me," he said. Theresa felt the pulse of the vein in
the side of Blake's neck. Her fingers rose and fell with the
strength of the beat.

"Listen, " he said, and drew her head to his chest. At
first, all she could hear was the rhythmic "thump-thump"
of his heart, a restless drum that seemed to vibrate even
the floor she was standing on. Theresa felt her heart speed
up and match the rhythm with its own beat.

"Listen," Blake said again. Theresa strained her ears. At
first it was a rushing sound, like being caught in the
middle of a river that flowed fast and deep. Then,
underneath the fury, Theresa heard the voices, hundreds

of voices. "Help me," some cried. "No," others moaned. The rest were sounds, sounds that started out as human and changed into a howl of pain and desperation, loss and emptiness, and finally a terrifying silence.

Theresa pulled her hand from Blake's neck and her head from his chest. She gasped as her heartbeat broke back into its own rhythm.

"No," she said, her voice low and thick in her throat. "I don't want you."

Blake nodded. He smoothed her hair from her face and pressed his cooling lips against her forehead. "Good," he said, and went back to the bedroom.

Theresa turned to the mirror, her face pale, her eyes filled with both fear and knowledge. The taste of her own blood was still on her tongue as she reached for her toothbrush. When her mouth was clean and the shirt back on the bathroom floor, Theresa went into the bedroom. Blake was under the covers, his hands straight out along his side.

As she did each morning, Theresa pulled down the shades and made sure the drapes were securely drawn. Blake was drowsy, his eyes barely able to open. The sun was minutes away from breaking the horizon. This was when they were the most vulnerable, Blake once told her. That time between sleep and wakefulness, when the edges of dreams start to fade and reality came into focus.

"If you ever want to kill me, do it then," he had said.

Theresa leaned across the bed and gazed at her husband's high forehead, the brow smooth and unlined. She tucked the comforter close around his body. Blake's eyes were closed now and his breathing barely perceptible. Theresa traced the outline of his mouth with her finger.

"Not yet," she whispered. "Not yet."

Symbiosis

Rhomylly B. Forbes

The city belonged to Graciela. No other of her kind had come forward to challenge that claim in a quarter of a century, perhaps longer. This was not unusual; it was primarily a matter of preserving one's territory. For the sake of custom and safety, one Child of the Night was quite sufficient for any major metropolitan area; more might arouse detection by the Children of the Day.

Consequently, the red flyer with gothic black lettering taped to the inner window of Dragon's Tears Bookstore announcing, "VampireCon! Celebrate the night and take over the Washington Hilton . . . For more information, call . . ." most certainly caught Graciela's attention.

Vampire . . . Con? In my city? Who dares?!? **Graciela thought, the unfamiliar emotions of worry and anger** wrinkling her smooth ivory brow. *No, it could not be so. I would sense . . . I shall go and teach these usurpers a lesson.* She set her mouth in a grimace. *They will learn that this is not their city . . . and that it is mine!*

Graciela's preternaturally sharp fangs flashed once in the light from a sputtering neon sign as she faded into the dark streets with a swiftness and agility born of long practice.

No one paid the slightest attention to the tall, pale woman in impeccably neat but somewhat old-fashioned garments, long auburn hair tumbling free about her waist, prowling about the lobby, ballrooms, and hallways of the Washington Hilton. Days later, when she had time to think on it, Graciela allowed herself a moment of surprise that she had, in fact, not attracted undue notice. Almost everyone else she encountered sported black, old-fashioned clothing, full black capes, and black hair—some obviously, and poorly, dyed.

But nowhere could Graciela smell another true Child of the Night.

What is this! A film! Not one of them is real. Graciela shrugged her shoulders as yet another youngster in badly-applied white pancake makeup and black eyeliner raced by. She had not hunted in two or three days. At her advanced age, Graciela no longer needed to drain her chosen victim to the point of death. However, most mortals were neither eager nor willing to "donate" the relatively small amount of fresh blood she occasionally needed to survive. This was a nice, clean hotel. It was unlikely there were any rats about.

But maybe, just maybe, she could make a fantasy come true for one of these pretenders. Graciela had read quite a bit of popular fiction about her own kind; she knew what humans desired, or at least what they purported to desire. Not that she had any intention of transforming her prey into a Child of the Night, but perhaps she might find and seduce an attractive, willing victim for a quick . . . taste. Tomorrow night, away from this bizarre parody, she would fully satisfy her mild hunger. Graciela chuckled low and deep, with a hint of irony. *But what a perfect place to hunt! These strange mortals masquerading as vampires do not recognize me as the real thing. And even if they did, they would likely beg me to perform the rite of blood sharing with them rather than attack me with a wooden stake. How completely odd. . . .*

Her mind resolved, Graciela decided to explore this strange gathering more thoroughly. Hundreds of years of honing a Child of the Night's natural swiftness and agility allowed her to enter a large, crowded place called "Huckster's Room" without the benefit of a "Con Badge." She puzzled over a display of small metal disks covered with writing that proclaimed KISS ME, I'M BATTY! and VAMPIRES DO YOU TILL YOU'RE SUCKED DRY and GO FANG YOURSELF. She had no idea what they meant, but they seemed very popular; there were more humans clustered around this booth than any other. Perhaps they were religious slogans of some sort.

A few tables sold clothing similar to what Graciela had seen on the humans in the hallway: full black capes, black wool pants, short black leather skirts, long black frock coats. In her soft burgundy velvet smoking jacket, crisp white tuxedo shirt (unbuttoned low enough to show a hint of cleavage), and faded blue jeans, Graciela felt positively underdressed. She looked down to find she was the only female there not shod in black pumps with stiletto heels. *How,* she wondered crazily, *could they ever catch their prey in those? I would fall down like a fool if I tried.* Graciela gazed fondly for a brief moment on her own worn but still sturdy black Reebok hi-tops. *Much more practical. Comfortable, too. If these mortals were true Children of the Night, they would starve within a week.*

A woman in the requisite black garb and white makeup walked up and asked her a question. "Excuse me?" Graciela asked politely. She had no little difficulty understanding what the woman was saying.

"I thaid," the woman lisped slowly. She wore some small plastic device in her mouth, giving her the appearance of having greenish-white fangs. It also made the woman spit horribly; Graciela desperately wanted to wipe her own face dry, but was afraid that would be considered rude. "Do you know when the danth ith thuppothed to thtart?"

"Death?"

"Danth! Danth! Wock and Woll! You know, dithco!" The woman had the nerve to look at Graciela as if she were the idiot.

"Oh, dance! Uh, no. No I do not. Sorry."

The woman shrugged. "Nithe fangth," she said as she moved away. "They look weal."

Real? Of course they're real! Oh, never mind. "Thank you," was all she said to the woman's retreating backside.

Graciela decided she'd had quite enough "Huckster's Room." She slipped into something called "Art Show" when the pale man in an ill-fitting tuxedo who was guarding the door became distracted by a wandering teenage girl covered only by a few sparse bands of leather and black spandex in strategic places.

Wandering the makeshift aisles of what she discovered was some sort of temporary gallery featuring very strange art, Graciela marveled anew at the fascination, sometimes obsession, that mortals had with her kind. She gaped in disbelief at a collection of cartoons featuring cute, furry ferrets with sharp fangs and black capes, wondering if she had missed some hidden profound message or meaning.

There were pictures of vampires sitting in front of computers, vampires flying spaceships, vampires watching television, even one of a vampire "moonbathing" in the nude.

I do not understand any of this at all. Why do these particular mortals . . . idolize us so? There is nothing glamorous about being a Child of the Night, nothing exciting. It is lonely, it is dangerous, it is . . . **Graciela** sighed, searching for the right word. *Empty.*

She came to the end of one of the aisles and stopped; the large oil painting hanging there immediately commanded all of her attention. Moonlight illuminated a tall, handsome, male vampire astride a black stallion. The vampire was kissing the hand of a lady vampire standing in the snow at the horse's side, her cape billowing in the cold night air. Both wore the tenderest expressions Graciela had ever seen on any face, mortal or no.

Long ago, when Graciela was a newly-made Child of the Night, she used to dream of such a scene as this. Love among her kind was a very rare thing, and she had quickly learned not to yearn for it. But this painting, the adoration depicted on the lady vampire's face, renewed those centuries-old desires. Suddenly Graciela ached with loneliness. Turning, she fled "Art Show" in blind sorrow with all the swiftness of which she was capable.

In the relative safety of the lobby, Graciela paused for a moment to restore her customary calm, then decided to peruse the smaller rooms down the hall from "Huckster's Room" and "Art Show." Perhaps a likely victim could be found there.

The first room contained a small group of people sitting crosslegged on the floor, paying rapt attention to a stocky, bearded man who looked and smelled as if he hadn't bathed in weeks. He was strumming a slightly out-of-tune guitar and everyone was singing:

> *And there was Brown, upside-down*
> *Hanging like a bat among the beams.*
> *"Blood! Blood!" the townsfolk cried*
> *As they filled our ears with screams.*
> *Oh, don't let 'em in til we've all drunk up.*
> *Somebody shouted "Hey Vampire!"*
> *HEY VAMPIRE!*
> *And we all sucked blue blind paralytic blood*
> *Til the castle walls caught fire.*

Graciela shuddered, and quickly closed the door behind her.

The next room was empty.

The third room was filled with very solemn looking people, all wearing formal, black clothing with accents of red and white. At the front of the room stood an imposing figure, pale as linen, with a black velvet robe and ropes of cheap garnets strung about his neck, presiding over a very nervous-looking couple.

As Graciela opened the door, the young lady was saying, "I, Akasha, take thee, Lestat, to be my lawfully undead husband. . . ." Graciela vaguely recalled reading some very popular books a few years ago that featured vampire characters with those names. She didn't remember much from the books, but was pretty certain that "Lestat" had weighed more than ninety pounds and usually wore pants with legs long enough to cover his bony shins. Also, if she recalled correctly, "Akasha" had neither blonde roots in her hair nor braces on her teeth. Graciela fled this room even more quickly than she had the singer's.

Now what? Graciela was pondering her next move when all of a sudden a horrific noise filled the hallway. It started as a strange metallic screech, then became a crash that was followed by something that sounded as if a dozen Siamese cats were being murdered.

The Undead Dance had officially begun.

Graciela peeped into the darkened banquet hall that had been pressed into service as a discotheque, unable to see much because of the strange flashing lights, artificial fog, and crowded, jiggling bodies. She circled the perimeter of the room and gazed at the wildly hopping dancers in stunned fascination. She was not paying much attention to where she was going.

"Oof! Oh, gosh, I'm so sorry!" The person she had just walked into had to yell to be heard above the unbearably loud music.

"No, please. It was my fault. I should have looked . . ." Graciela bellowed in response until a careful look at the person made the words falter and die in her throat.

It was a young woman in her mid-twenties, with unruly blond curls that tumbled past her shoulders, and a body that would have made Rubens fall to his knees and pray for permission to paint it. Unlike practically everyone else Graciela had seen so far, she was dressed in clothing that actually fit. It also flattered her solid frame, although the long, full, rust-colored skirt topped by a complementing floral lace-up bodice was hardly daily street wear, at least for these times. The ivory peasant blouse underneath the girl's bodice drooped seductively off her ample shoulders, nicely exposing her cleavage and the top of her soft breasts. Graciela felt faint stirrings of hunger, both for blood and . . . well, Graciela hadn't felt stirrings for that in over two centuries.

But she was certainly feeling them now.

And she had no idea what to do.

Fortunately, the young mortal saved the situation. "Wanna dance?" she shrieked.

Dance? Me? Like that? I . . . I don't know how. I'll look foolish. I have no sense of rhythm. Ohhh, how did I ever get myself into this? Graciela took a deep breath and hollered the only thing she could, under the circumstances. "Yes. I would like to dance."

They moved out onto the floor, amid a sea of bouncing, jerking bodies. To her eternal relief, Graciela found that her dance moves looked no more awkward than anyone else's. In fact, once she relaxed and actually listened to the music, she started to enjoy herself.

The next number was a slow, romantic ballad, and before Graciela could even think, the young woman was snuggled in her arms, her head nestled trustingly on Graciela's shoulder. Graciela could feel the girl's breasts crushed against her own chest, and somehow, even through the many layers of clothing the girl was wearing, Graciela could feel a heat, a need, emanating from her groin. At the end of the number, Graciela lifted the girl's chin with her finger and kissed her long and slow and deep, gently cupping the human's face in her hands and taking care not to let her sharp fangs hurt the girl. Not yet.

In the quiet lull between the end of the song and the beginning of the next one the girl said, "My name's Joanie. Would you like to go somewhere quiet—to, um, talk?"

Graciela was beginning to get a little confused. *I thought I was supposed to be the hunter, here. This girl— Joanie?—is making all the first moves, and I'm letting her!* "I would like that very much." She followed the blond human out of the hot, noisy banquet hall.

"I have a room here at the hotel, if you'd like . . ." Joanie was blushing slightly.

"That would be fine." If vampires had that ability, she'd be blushing also. *This is ridiculous! What is going on here?*

As they waited for the elevator, Joanie asked, "What's your name?"

"Graciela."

"Pretty. French?"

"No. Italian, actually." *What am I doing! I never give my real name to prey, much less tell them where I come from!*

Joanie reached over and gently laced her warm fingers around Graciela's cool ones. They entered the lift, still holding hands.

Joanie's hotel room was at the very end of a well-lit, carpeted hallway. On the way from the elevator they passed several rooms whose open doors revealed loud, raucous gatherings. Graciela had heard the term "party animal." A few glances at the individuals attending the gatherings taught her its meaning.

Mercifully, the heavy, closed door of Joanie's room muffled most of the sound. Joanie quickly walked over to a rather large portable object that Graciela knew was commonly called a "boom box." "Do you like classical?"

"What?" As her experience with hotel rooms was rather limited, Graciela was taking the opportunity to explore her surroundings. At the moment she was trying not to wrinkle her nose in distaste at the ugly, impersonal decor and disinfectant smell. "Oh. Yes. I like classical."

Joanie touched a button on the box's surface and the opening bars of Beethoven's Egmont Overture filled the space, effectively masking the remaining sounds of Bacchanalian revels from the hallway.

"Nice."

"Thank you." *Stop stalling, Joanie! You know what you brought her here for!*

Graciela caught a glimpse of herself in the mirror. Even allowing for a Child of the Night's natural pallor, she looked **pale and nervous.** *Stop stalling, Graciela! You know what you brought her here for!*

"I . . ." they both said at once. Joanie recovered first. She let out a soft chuckle, and opened her arms invitingly. "Come."

With a low moan, Graciela crossed the room to take her place in Joanie's embrace. She lowered her lips to meet the girl's, her hands buried in Joanie's thick curls. Graciela cradled the human in one powerful arm, with her other hand she loosened the front lacings of Joanie's bodice, her fingers deft and sure even though it had been many centuries since she had handled such clothing.

Never had Joanie experienced such a kiss. It made the one they'd shared on the dance floor seem fleeting, shallow, in comparison. She closed her eyes and let herself thoroughly explore Graciela's mouth, her tongue and teeth, and allowed Graciela to explore hers in turn. She felt as if her very soul were being pulled into that kiss.

Joanie reached up and began to tug at Graciela's jacket until it was a small pile of burgundy velvet on the carpet. Joanie's bodice soon followed. Without the bodice to hold it up, her peasant blouse fell almost to her waist, baring firm yet ample breasts and full, pink nipples. Joanie quickly unbuttoned Graciela's white, pleated shirt, and allowed it to join the other garments on the floor. She grabbed Graciela by the shoulders and gently but firmly pushed her down until she was sitting on the edge of the bed, then swiftly removed her own skirt and blouse. A few moments later, Graciela's sneakers and jeans were added to the pile of discarded clothing.

Before Graciela had a chance to protest, much less assume control of the rapidly evolving situation, she found herself lying naked in Joanie's arms, her skin tingling from the feather-light kisses Joanie was planting all over her body. Within moments, Joanie began to gently

knead, nibble and lick Graciela's firm white breasts and
light brown nipples, and for the first time in over two
hundred years, Graciela groaned softly with desire.

Slowly, tormentingly slowly, Joanie kissed and licked
and suckled her way down to the soft crease between
Graciela's thighs and torso, missing not an inch. Pink skin
mingled freely with alabaster as Joanie gently spread
Graciela's thighs and settled herself comfortably between
the vampire's long, muscular legs. Joanie teased the top
and inside of Graciela's thighs with her soft pink tongue,
swooping down every so often to brush the outside of the
vampire's nether lips, making Graciela clutch the thin
bedspread beneath her with rock-hard fingers. Before she
could stop herself, Graciela began to writhe and twist her
hips, desperately trying to make Joanie's tongue touch her
long-neglected clitoris by accident. It didn't work.

"Please," Graciela whispered, too consumed by need to
care that she, the superior being, was begging a mortal for
sexual release. "Oh, please."

Joanie gently parted Graciela's outer lips with her
fingers and began to lap softly at the unusually salty but
not unpleasant nectar she found there, before working her
way up to the vampire's hardened button. As Joanie's
tongue made first contact with that sensitive nub,
Graciela gasped. Joanie flicked her tongue hard and fast
against Graciela's clitoris, then changed the rhythm to
soft and slow, licking the area on either side of Graciela's
tiny organ with her firm tongue before sliding back down
to her sweet opening for another taste and driving
Graciela nearly wild and to the brink of orgasm in the
process.

Joanie sensed that her new lover was on that edge,
because she pulled back and lightened her tongue touch,
forcing Graciela to push up with her hips to maintain any
contact at all, until at last Joanie took pity on her and

plunged her moistened face back into Graciela's warm slit, licking it with a fury until Graciela reached a shattering release, arching her body off the bed and nearly breaking Joanie's nose by accident on the strength of her bucking hips alone.

When Graciela could see again, Joanie was holding her gently in her arms and looking somewhat smug. "Long time?"

A brief, sorrowful look crossed the vampire's features. "Longer than you could know." Then she brightened. "So . . . ?"

Without another word, Joanie grinned happily and settled back on the thin comforter. Starting at the tops of Joanie's feet, Graciela kissed, caressed, explored, and gently licked her way up the girl's body. Joanie tried not to giggle when Graciela reached her kneecaps, but it did tickle a little.

Graciela found and lightly caressed every sensitive spot: the inside of Joanie's elbows, the small of her back, pausing her intense explorations every so often to tease Joanie's nipples to erection with lips and tongue. *Amazing. I haven't forgotten how to satisfy a human woman after all. Although I cannot recall that any of the others satisfied me first. . . . I could easily grow accustomed to that. . . .*

And whenever any part of Graciela's magnificent body was in reach, Joanie's fingers and mouth were busy exploring also. Joanie discovered that Graciela had a particularly erogenous spot at the base of her spine, and another one right above her left hip. Thigh, stomach, and breast, light tan and pale ivory, all blended together to form a wondrous whole.

Graciela could sense the musky dampness gathering between Joanie's legs. Slowly, almost teasingly, she slid down the girl's body, nudged her legs apart and gently spread her moist, rosy labia and began to circle Joanie's clitoris with sensuous thumb strokes, sometimes trading it for tongue and lips in the oldest act of love she knew. Joanie's breathing was becoming heavy and ragged when Graciela smoothly shifted position, her mouth positioned over the curve formed by the union of Joanie's neck and shoulder, leaving her fingers to coax even more sweet honey from Joanie's warm slit. Graciela's hunger for blood was almost as strong as Joanie's need for orgasm at that moment. *Yesss. It is time.*

"Oh, yes!" Joanie growled, turning her head and brushing a few stray curls away to expose the vulnerable area further. "Take me! Oh, bite me, please!"

Graciela' fingers increased the rhythm and pressure on Joanie's throbbing nub and slowly, delicately, pierced the tender pink throat flesh with her needle-sharp teeth. Instead of struggling or fainting like all of Graciela's previous prey, Joanie screamed Graciela's name in ecstasy. The familiar, warm waves of orgasm rocked her body as she clutched Graciela's head to her shoulder and held on for dear life, her soul dancing in joyous oblivion.

The sudden rush of pure orgasmic energy that poured into Graciela via Joanie's blood completely satisfied the vampire's hunger even more quickly than usual. Confused and slightly embarrassed, she pulled back shortly after Joanie relaxed in post-release contentment, unwilling to meet the girl's earnest gray eyes. Joanie languidly lifted one hand to her neck, staring in mild amazement when the fingers came away smeared with blood.

"So. Now you know." Graciela rose from the bed and began to rummage about on the floor for her clothing, intending to dress and flee the girl's presence as quickly as she was able. It was a large city; she was a very old, highly skilled vampire. The girl would never see her again and, in time, would most likely relegate this entire episode to the realm of dream, or fantasy, or both, and Graciela would once again be alone. But Joanie's soft words stopped her.

"I already did."

It is not easy to surprise an eight-hundred-year-old Child of the Night, but Joanie had just done it. Graciela quickly sat down in an overstuffed chair, clutching her smoking jacket about her like a shawl. Joanie slowly eased herself up until she was sitting against the padded headboard, resplendent in her nakedness and terrified of saying the wrong thing that would drive this exquisite creature from her life forever. Graciela took a deep breath. "How?"

"Three things, actually. The biggest clue came when we were kissing earlier. I've seen a lot of custom-carved fangs in my time, but I've always been able to see, or at least feel, the seams where they fit over the person's real canine teeth. Yours don't have any seams. Plus, your skin is too cold and too white for you to be anything else."

"And the other?"

Joanie's eyes grew soft and even more compassionate. "I noticed you earlier in the Art Show, and I saw how you reacted to my painting."

"Your painting?" Graciela was confused.

Joanie gestured to a scattered pile of matted prints covering the top of the low dresser. "I'm a semiprofessional artist. That's why I'm here. That large oil painting, it's one of mine. Most people see it as the ultimate fantasy; you saw it as a shattered reality. I could tell by your face."

Graciela nodded and swallowed—hard. "Why . . . why did you paint it?"

"I'm not sure. It's part of why I'm attracted to the whole vampire role-playing subculture, I guess."

Finally, the chance to ask the one question Graciela had been aching to ask a human for years. "And why is that?"

Joanie smiled and snorted softly. "There's probably as many answers to that as there are humans playing the life. For me. . . ." She paused for a moment, trying to find the right words to explain. "My parents died when I was a little girl, and I was handed around from relative to relative while I was growing up. I've always been attracted to vampirism because it seemed to have such a strong sense of . . . permanence, I guess, something I needed pretty desperately. Also, the idea of not dying and not losing any more loved ones to death also had—has—a lot of appeal." Joanie started to blush. "Plus, as you've seen, I have some, ah, unusual tastes in lovemaking."

"Women?"

"Well, that too, but I meant, um, being bitten. Blood."

"Oh."

"Speaking of which, are you sure you, how do I say this, got enough?"

It is even harder to surprise an eight-hundred-year-old Child of the Night twice, but Joanie had just done it again. "You enjoyed that?"

Joanie's smile looked quite satisfied. "Oh God, yes! You couldn't tell?" Graciela shook her head no, too dumbfounded to speak. "I've gotta tell you—your teeth didn't even really hurt. Not like a human's at all. In fact, I was kinda hoping we could do it again sometime. Soon. Often." She looked at Graciela pleadingly and was surprised to see the vampire's dark brown eyes well up with blood-tinged tears. Joanie leaped off the bed and knelt at Graciela's feet, gently covering the hands that were still clutching the smoking jacket. "What's the matter? Did I say something wrong?"

"No." Graciela wiped her eyes, then wiped them again. "I am not accustomed to bringing such happiness, such pleasure to my prey. It is not the usual way of my kind. I would . . . I would very much like to share lovemaking with you again." *And for a brief while, my little Golden One, I will not be alone, I will not be empty. This is too much to hope for.* "But I do not understand. You wish me in your life?"

It was Joanie's turn to become teary-eyed. She nodded. "I . . . this sounds silly, I know, but I've dreamed about finding someone like you for a long time. Let's just take things one day, oops, sorry, one night at a time and see how it goes. What do you say?"

Graciela smiled, the first time she could remember doing so in decades. "I say yes. But tell me, Joanie," The name was already a caress upon her still-bloodstained lips. "From what I have read and all I have seen tonight, I am surprised you do not immediately ask for the rite of blood sharing. Why is this?"

Joanie paused for a minute, then an impish grin slowly spread over her features. "Well, don't you think it would be kinda foolish to ask to spend eternity with you when we don't even know if you can get along with my cat?"

And even an eight-hundred-year-old vampire had to acknowledge the wisdom of that.

El Tigre

Catherine Lundoff

I have but recently arrived in this new land, sent from my home in disgrace for believing the seductive words of a young noble from the court. He took advantage of my naivete, and now both my child and I will pay the price: she raised as a bastard in the convent in Spain, and I sent to this cursed land conquered by barbarians who call themselves my country-men. I was told that I am to be the new "companion" (a term that I believe to be synonymous with "maid") to a Doña Fernanda, a widow related somehow to the Viceroy, as well as distantly related to my cousins and myself. It is hoped by my cousins, the only family that I possess, that here in Mexico, far from my disgrace, I will find a suitable marriage. I hate them all.

Closing my diary, I find my gaze drawn out out the
window to the courtyard below. Dimly lit archways open
onto a dusty open patio, circled by some small orange
trees, with an even smaller central fountain, a sad replica
of the great palaces of the Moors in my beloved Spain. I
lean on the edge of the window, inhaling the warm
evening air in great breaths as I try not to weep. A noise
below causes me to pull back into the shadows. In the
dusk, I see a cloaked figure emerge from one of the
archways on the floor below and walk swiftly toward the
stables. Surely it is some other servant of the elusive Doña
Fernanda, whom I have yet to meet in my two days here.
A servant on an errand, yes, that's it; thus, I try to dismiss
my curiosity. But my gaze follows the figure as he
emerges, leading a black horse, mounts, and rides rapidly
from the courtyard. What errand could call for sending a
man out onto the dirt roads outside of Veracruz, just as
night falls?

I ponder this question as I draw the shutters closed.
There are many such thoughts for me to mull over, first
and foremost concerning the purpose of serving as a
"companion" to a woman I have not seen. At least my
room is plain and comfortable—far from luxurious, but
better than the convent. The bed, with its carved wooden
posts, seems large enough for two, and there is a strange
and beautiful woven cloth draped over the wardrobe
which holds my attention each time I approach it.

I bow my head for the prayers that do not come before
the image of the Santa María which rests on the carved
wooden shelf on the wall opposite from my bed. Then,
placing my rosary on the shelf before her statue, I read the
Bible in the wide bed with its woven coverlet until I fall
asleep, one of the few things that I can thank the nuns for
teaching me. I wake with a gasp many hours later, my
nightdress open at the throat, shivering in the night

breezes from the open window. *But surely I closed that,* I think to myself as I dash across the room to shut it again.

It is only when I return to the large soft bed that I remember my dream. A dream about a woman, wearing the clothing of a man(!), standing over my bed, and gazing down at me. She is tall and lean, wearing a long black cloak and carrying a sword. Her high cheekbones and long black hair mark her as *mestiza,* one whom my countrymen see as "tainted" with the blood of the unfortunate indios of this land. She is beautiful and even in my memory, I am drawn to her. Drawn to her, perhaps, more strongly than to the young lord whose words brought me here. I find that I want to taste her lips, as thoughts that had been carefully forced down in the convent return once more. I remember lusting after Sister Teresa, the strongest and most comely of the nuns, remember desiring her attention, even her punishments. Here is another such a one to awaken that desire I thought long dead within me.

My awareness shifts as her hand brushes my hair away from my face in this dream of mine, the most vivid I have had in some time. As her hands brush my face and neck, I find my lips caressing them. I blush somewhat to think of it, but only a little, for I am a fallen woman, even at only eighteen summers, not some convent innocent who has never known carnal desires.

I draw her onto the bed in this vision of mine, reaching out to pull her lips to mine for a kiss. Even though it is just a dream, I feel the heat rush through me as I remember the imagined touch of her lips. Her lips part and she showers my neck with kisses, as she unfastens the top of my nightdress to expose more of my shoulders and neck. In this dream, I know that I will give her anything she wants, though I should burn in Hell for eternity as the priests told me. I feel her bite my shoulder, then a dreamy lassitude overtakes me and I fall into a deeper sleep.

Having remembered, I lie awake until the first birdsong drives me from my bed to gaze out the window.

My hands go to my shoulder and looking down, I can see a bruise with two small cuts where I was unmarked the night before. I shiver superstitiously and cross myself more from habit than belief. The sainted *iglesia Católica* never did aught for me but tell me that women who bore bastards were doomed in the hereafter. Nevertheless, I fear this unknown mark as I fear the heat that she awoke. I try to pray as the only comfort left to me, but find that my thoughts will turn only to the night before and to my daughter.

The tears come, unwanted, when I think upon my little one back in Spain and the fact that I will never see her again. That thought pains me more than the realization that I am alone and unprotected in a new land, with strange marks upon my shoulder. I hastily wipe my eyes as one of the servants enters silently to tell me that the Doña will see me after I have eaten my evening meal. She exits swiftly back into the hall.

It strikes me as odd that all of the Doña's other servants are so very quiet, so sullen, so quick to disappear. The majority are old women, with craggy unsmiling faces, garbed always in black, much like this one. Perhaps the Doña's household is still in mourning. What must this woman be like to rule such a house of sorrow? My curiosity consumes me and the day passes slowly until my dinner arrives. I eat the odd mixture of rice and beans quickly and put on my most respectable dress, the finest of the plain black serge dresses that my cousins let me take when I departed. I wear it without adornment in deference to the house, then after a moment's thought, I defiantly fasten my black lace mantilla about my head and shoulders. The lace was my mother's, the last bit of luxury I was able to hide from the voracious hands of my cousins; I will not have the Doña think I have no pride at all. I leave to follow the servant to meet my new mistress.

I am escorted to a room, lit by a single candle, at the back of the house, one without windows in the dried clay walls. The candle barely illuminates the colorful carpet, the heavy wood furnishings and the room's only other occupant. She is heavily veiled, wearing a black silk dress trimmed with lace, and seated in a ornately carved wooden chair. I cannot not see her face as I make the appropriate curtsey, and so I study her curiously, in a manner that many have found impertinent. Somehow, I sense that she finds it amusing. "So," Doña Fernanda's deep voice fills the room, "you are sent to me from our shared cousins in Spain, and I am to feed you, house you, and find a match for you." I nod miserably. "And what will you do for me?" I know now that she is laughing at me.

Indignantly, I raised my head. "I can read and write, as well as play the harpsichord and other instruments. I'm sure my lady will find my abilities to be quite satisfactory."

"Good." That voice behind the veils purrs at me, and I feel a rise of that same heat that I felt last night and once again this morning. I gasp in horror and glance down quickly in hopes of covering my confusion. "I am ill much of the time, which forces me to rest during the day as it is much too hot for me. I would like to see you in the evenings, at which time you can entertain me. Once I get to know you better, we'll see about a match for you. Meanwhile, I suggest frequent baths to keep off the heat. The climate differs greatly from Spain." She rises to press my hand gently. I am dismissed, thinking as I leave that she does not seem much like an invalid.

Several days and interminable nights pass in which I am not sent for to be companionable, or otherwise. I read on the patio, attempt to gossip with the other servants, and wonder if my dream will come again. The others are not forthcoming about our mistress, saying only that she is a widow, whose husband died several years before. The Viceroy granted her permission to keep her husband's land and to not remarry, highly unusual in this land where wealthy widows are courted assiduously. I wonder how she did it, and whether I will be foisted off on one of her unsuccessful suitors. I long for more details about this woman who weighs so on my mind.

While I learn little about the mysterious Doña, they do tell me about another local mystery: a strange masked man, known as "El Tigre," who has been paying nightly visits to some of the more notoriously brutal landowners in the region. It is said that they are much kinder to the indios and peasants who work their land after such visits. Having heard something of the unchecked abuse by both Church and nobles, this news gladdens my heart. Perhaps he will rescue me from my boredom and disgrace, along with his other good deeds. Or, I dare to dream in my most secret depths, *she* will return.

In my boredom, I begin to take advantage of the Doña's library, where I read many interesting and surprising works. Among the most interesting things of course, is the existence of the library in the first place. Ordinarily, a wealthy woman in my country would possess only the Bible, and would be fortunate to be able to read that. *She must have been brought up by the nuns as well,* I think, *or else blessed with a remarkable parent.* One of the works that holds my attention is a tome on the forces of darkness, and how they operate in the mortal world. I read about demons and succubi, about creatures who steal infants, and about those who seduce men in their sleep. I cannot help but wonder if my dream lady is one of them, but I can find no reference to such a female demon visiting a mortal woman.

I also begin to bathe in the sunken pool downstairs provided for that purpose, as I had been advised. One night, as I lie soaking in my thin, white shift, as all good girls are supposed to do, something the nuns told me often enough, I hear someone enter. Thinking it to be the quiet housemaid, Consuelo, with more hot water, I murmur "Gracías." The chuckle that answers is certainly not Consuelo, and my startled eyes open to find the Doña kneeling next to the pool near my head. Immediately I am torn between wanting her to find me irresistible and wanting to conceal my body, made very visible by the wet shift.

Years of convent training make me draw myself up, instinctively covering myself with my hands. As I sit up, she tilts my head back, and lifting her veil, presses her lips to mine. My wet arm slides from over my breasts and goes around her neck of its own accord, as though I am possessed, as perhaps I am. I feel her hand move down to cup my breast and to caress my nipple. The nuns' distant voices shriek warnings of the eternal flames as my flesh burns to her touch, and I respond, racing far beyond their reach.

My delighted gasp is permission enough for her, and she pulls me onto the towels next to the pool. I am amazed at her strength. In the dim light, I cannot not see her face very well, but her kisses tell me that she is the woman from my dream. I draw back in amazement to study her cold, fierce beauty. "I have dreamt of you. . . ." I whisper.

"No dream, little one. I could not stay away from your beauty. I have known that I must have you since I first saw your portrait and heard your tale. But you must know that I am not like you. Even my very distant cousins would not have deliberately delivered you into the power of a demon." Demon? I study her avidly, heart racing, knowing I must seem wild-eyed with terror.

"I am not mortal, dulce. I will live forever, surviving on the blood of others. The warm light of the sun is death to me, so I must sleep during the days and move about only in the dark. I have been this way for many years, after my husband's bite brought me over." She pauses distastefully on the word *husband*. "I knew nothing of what he was about, having been a convent bred innocent, much like you, *amor*. He fed off me until I became as I am now. I learned enough to hasten his end in revenge for making me a monster. I also learned to savor the joys of a woman's body from one of his erstwhile loves and realized that I was not ready to be completely dead. Now, I find that I am lonely, and longing for the warmth of a mortal lover. But I will not deceive you as I was deceived." She turns to me, eyes glowing,"Will you share my bed, knowing what I am and what I can do?"

My hand strays to my neck, to the marks she left in my dream vision, now made stark and real. "I must draw deeper than that, amor, draining you close to dry before you become as I am. If I terrify you, you have only to say the word and I will find you a husband. I am nothing if not honorable." She smiles a strange, sad, twisted smile. I reach out to that sorrow. *What are we both but women with naught except each other?* I draw her hand back to my bosom.

Her hands are on the strings of my shift, and I am lost in the soft touch of her lips, her tongue as she kisses my neck. Soon my shift is down around my waist and her mouth is on my breast. I feel my back bend as her tongue strokes over my nipples. My hands scrabble at the fastenings on the back of her dress, wanting her to be as vulnerable as I am. She evades me, sliding the wet shift lower as she lays me down on the towels.

She licks her way along my legs, and I am filled with a desperate sense of desire and panic. *What is she doing to me?* Her tongue reaches the space between my legs and I scream with delight, with horror as she sends flames through me. *Truly I am damned now,* I think, *but if this is Hell, Heaven can be no better.* I am swept along by the strokes of her tongue until all my muscles bend at once and I must cry out. She licks her way back up to my mouth and I see that her eyes are larger and darker than any others I have seen before. I pull her to me, but not before I notice something else. Her teeth are long and sharp, and I gasp in terror, marveling that I had not noticed them before. Torn between fear and lust, I hold her off me for a moment. "Do you mean to kill me?" I manage to ask.

"I mean to possess you completely." Her eyes mesmerize me and I fall into them, not caring if she drains me dry or if such desires will cast me from the Church forever. I feel her teeth graze my neck, and I bend my head back so she can reach me, can drink my blood though it means my life. Her teeth sink in and I feel some pain, then a joyous lethargy as I slip into a deep sleep.

I wake somewhat tired, but gloriously happy in the late morning light. If this is what it means to be a "companion," then I shall regret only the loss of my daughter, and nothing else. I do realize that it will not do for the servants to see her love bites on my neck, and I wrap a silken cloth around my throat. Once again, some days pass before I see her again. The others, particularly Consuelo who has served her lady for a long time, warn me not to disturb her during the day, and she does not come to me at night for two nights. *Do I want to be as she is?* I cannot answer this question, and so I am in a fever of impatience, barely sleeping or eating for dreaming of her, yet torn with fear, for I, too, am not ready to be completely dead.

As I stand near the window on the second night lit up by the full moon, I see the cloaked figure once again leaving the house to go toward the stables. One glance and I know it is she, so strong and purposeful is her stride. With no thought as to why she would ride at night, I run downstairs in my shift with nothing over me but a silken shawl. I reach the patio just as she leads the horse from the stables. "Take me with you!" I gasp. "I cannot, my love." I see that she is dressed in men's clothing, wearing a sword and a mask, and I realize who el Tigre must be. I plant myself before her, and without a second thought, I tear my shift open at the neck in hope that my offer will be enough, for I know that men hunt for el Tigre and I fear for her as much as I want her.

She growls and her arms encircle me, lips pressed so hard against mine that my lips feel bruised. "I must feed elsewhere lest I kill you. When I feed from the landowners, I can terrify them into treating the peasants better," she whispers into my ear as she kisses it, her hands running over my body under the shawl, in spite of her words.

"I'll guard your horse and wait for you," I whisper. "Please. I don't want any more nights without you."

She studies me for a long moment, eyes midnight pools that I drown in, long, lithe body graceful and powerful in her man's garb. Finally, with a dry laugh, she swings onto the horse, pulling me up before her and wrapping the cloak around us both. "Very well, dulce. I would be pleased to savor your charms before this evening's less pleasant task." Her arms encircle me while her hands rip the shift further until one of her hands cups my breast. I arch my head backward onto her shoulder gasping as the heat fills me.

The horse takes us where it will, until I look around to realize that it has come to a stop and we are in an old cemetery, some distance from her hacienda. Tall, dark trees surround the stones marking the graves of the dead. It is a strange, macabre sight, lit only by the moon. Some of the stones lay at odd angles as though the dead themselves had shifted them and I shiver at the thought. "Does this spot frighten you, amor? I feel a special kinship to it, and it is undisturbed by those who seek el Tigre. I will take you home if it is too much," she murmurs in my ear.

Something about this place of the dead draws me as well, in spite of my terrors. Suddenly I find that I desire her touch her here, with the eyes of the ghosts upon on us. "I fear nothing while I am with you, mi amor," I whisper in a voice scarcely my own, as I place my hand on hers and hold it to my breast.

She pulls her hand away, leaps from the saddle, then lifts me down to the ground. As I touch her waist, I feel the coil of a long whip at her belt. Without thinking, even as she unclasps her cloak to lay it on a long flat gravestone, I pull the braided leather from her belt. My eyes close as I think back to the convent, to the many beatings that I received from Sister Teresa, to the look on the nun's face as the leather hit my skin and to the way her hands felt as she touched me afterward. I did many things to earn those beatings and that touch. Perhaps . . . I turn to Fernanda, holding the whip out. "I was very wicked to follow you the way I did," I whisper.

Her sharp teeth flash in the moonlight. "Oh, I must remember to thank those cousins of ours for such a wicked companion as they have found me. I have longed for a lover who would indulge all my desires of her own free will." The whip snakes along the ground as she turns me to face a standing tombstone. She shreds the shift from me and forces my legs further apart with her knee. I am not so much breathing as I am panting, like a dog, but I do not care. Nor do I feel the cold, even as her first stroke pushes me forward so that my breasts touch the icy stone. My head hangs over the stone as I embrace it. The whip snaps along my back; the burning of my skin and the burning in my belly becoming as one. My cries fill the night.

Five strokes and I can barely stand. I feel her stand behind me and run the handle of the whip up my legs. My moans and whimpers are beyond any restraint that I feel capable of exercising. I feel her lick the small amount of blood that she has drawn off my back as the whip handle slides further. She bends me further over the stone and slips it inside me. As she begins to thrust, my knees buckle and she has to hold me against her as she pushes the whip in and out of me. This is what I always dreamed that Sister Teresa would do, and I am crying, begging for more, begging for I know not what until my whole body can take no more and only her strong arms are holding me upright.

She picks me up and puts me on her cloak, her teeth finding my neck. I manage to unfasten her shirt to touch her breasts as she feeds. She pulls her bloody teeth from my neck as I wrap my legs around her waist. "I must feed elsewhere tonight, *querida mía*. I do not altogether trust myself with you." Dragging herself from me with an effort, she wraps the cloak around me. "Wait here. I'll return within the hour. Sleep." At her last word, I slip into that great abyss that such nights with her produce. Before I sleep, I think I see a great gray wolf running from the cemetery and down the road.

When I wake, I am in my own bed at the house. I wonder if I have dreamt it all until I feel the stripes on my back. For a brief moment, I am afraid that I have gone too

far, that she will kill me in her passion. The thought fills
me with only a vague apprehension, something which
puzzles me. Does my own life mean so little to me, that
losing it is nothing? Or do I trust her, a creature of the
night, not even mortal, so much that I will place my life
in her hands?

I contemplate how little I know of her, of her life and
what she is. I think back also on what my life had to offer
before her: disgrace, at best a joyless marriage, at worst a
life of dependency upon more fortunate relatives. As I
have only my daughter in all the world that I care about
other than her, and if I cannot have my little one back, I
throw my lot in with Doña Fernanda. Alive, with some
small measure of independence, I might yet think of some
way to regain my daughter.

With the matter settled for the moment in my own
mind, I eat well and rest, saving myself up for my beloved.
Somehow, I find that I do not greatly question that I
should love another woman, probably because I had seen
instances before, in the convent, that led me to believe
that such things were possible. She has certainly proven
on my own body that she can make me feel as I have
never felt before.

Some nights later, I am called to play the harpsichord
for Fernanda and some guests who have come from the
surrounding haciendas. She sends word of this by
Consuelo rather than coming herself, but at least she
sends a note as well. The note says, "Querida, I ask your
help in entertaining some of my kinswomen. Much will
be asked of you tonight. If you wish to please me, leave off
your heavy undergarments when you come to me. Trust
me and remember that I have some control over both
myself and others." I dress in an agony of apprehension
and anticipation.

When I enter the room, I see four women, two resembling Fernanda in some way that I only dimly comprehend. I sense, rather than identify, their kinship to her, knowing instinctively that they are like her and that the other two are mortal like me. They are all older than I, and wear the plain, simple garments of spinsters living on their family's largesse. Yet, I am drawn to their power and grace. These are not the sullen, broken women I am accustomed to seeing in wealthy households, but instead are like the abbess of the convent, both comfortable in their strength and somehow otherworldly.

We dine and the others study me almost as assiduously as I examine them. We exchange pleasantries and learn somewhat of each other; the others are all dueñas and companions, unmarried women and widows as I had suspected. The evening meal with its oddly flavored chicken and rice passes quickly. Once we have finished dining, Fernanda dismisses the servants and bolts the doors securely behind them. Smiling mysteriously, she ushers me to the harpsichord.

After I play, which I find makes me more homesick than I expected, Fernanda draws near and gently strokes my hair.

"You look sad, dulce. What is it?"

With little regard for the others who are tactfully engrossed in their own conversation, it tumbles from my mouth, "I love you, but I miss my daughter."

"Where is she?" asks Fernanda as though she has always known. Perhaps our cousins had told her.

"In the convent of the Santa María near Madrid," I offer in a rush.

"We will see what can be done. Now, would you like to help me entertain our guests?"

My heart fills with hope as I gaze up at her. "Anything you want of me, you are welcome to take, even my life."

"I don't want to take your life, but I desire you, your passion, your beauty. I want my friends to see the beauty of your body and your surrender as well," she whispers. "Oh, yes! Take me now!" I find the words pouring from my mouth, any thought of propriety long forgotten. She sits beside me on the playing bench, her hands unlacing the bodice confining my bosom. I hear a gasp from one of the other ladies as Fernanda bares my breast, then bends to take it into her mouth. My arms encircle her neck, frantic moans arising from me as I slip beyond self control. The thought of the other women watching makes me burn with desire, rather than the shame that I should feel.

I gaze back at them in time to see one of the women pull another to the floor in front of her, turning her so she can watch us, and sliding her hand into the other's bodice. I see the second one's look as the questing hand finds her nipple and she moans as she meets my eyes. I am wearing only a flimsy shift under my dress. Fernanda's hands pull the dress off me, leaving me in my light shift to face the women across the room. The woman caressing the other's breasts pulls a sharp dagger from the table and slices the second woman's dress from her with not a scratch. We face each other, each watching the other's excitement as the other two women watching begin to touch each other as well.

As my beloved's hands undress me, she reveals to the others that I am suffering from the curse of Eve. Pulling the rag from between my legs, she growls deep in her throat, and the others draw near, pulled to my blood. Before I can think more about it, Fernanda kneels between my legs and begins to lick me ferociously. Her two kinswomen hover nearby, their companions forgotten for the moment. The thrill of fear only makes the flames within me burn hotter. They could tear me limb from limb at this moment and I could do nothing to stop them. Fernanda lifts her head to gaze at me, eyes burning and mouth bloody. "Share," hisses one of the other women.

She favors them with a sharp-toothed smile. "Are you afraid, little one?" she asks, looking at me. I nod, too overcome to speak. "Do you want them anyway?" I nod my assent again and she moves to hold me as another takes her place. The two human women hover nearby, watching and touching each other, too overcome to resist the sight of my pleasure. The fierce tongue drives me harder and harder until I cry out as my body arches out of control. The third moves to take her place as the second lady returns to the two companions. I hear their moans mixed with my own. My hands grasp her hair as she feeds. Fernanda's fingers tighten on my breast as she kisses me, her tongue inside my mouth. Once again I am transported, crying out into Fernanda's mouth as that insistent tongue strokes and slides inside me and against me. The other woman sits up panting, my blood on her fangs.

She watches me for a moment more, then bows to Fernanda and moves to join the others; plainly, she commands them. One of the human women has pinned the arms of the other, now stripped of her dress, while one of the vampire ladies caresses and kisses her. She begs and moans, arching her back and opening her legs to express her desire but the kissing and biting continues. The sight arouses me again and I reach for my beloved. Her fingers slide inside me. Her other hand turns my face toward the women as one of them pulls a leather belt from her dress and begins to lightly smack the bared legs and back of the woman who is now kneeling before her. I squirm against Fernanda and she pinches my breasts hard. "You're very wicked to want another, my sweet," she growls in my ear.

She pulls me from the bench and across the room in a single movement. I am pushed to my knees, my face between the legs of the woman I have just seen whipped. "Lick!" Fernanda's order could not be denied, and I taste another woman for the first time. The belt's sharp smack on my buttocks distracts me for a moment, only to have the woman catch my head and pull my face back into her. "I'll stop if you don't please her." This threat serves only to inspire me further. As the sting of the belt warms me, I move my hand up to her, part her with my fingers and push inside as Fernanda did to me. Her fierce cries of joy warm me until I beg for my loved one's touch, her hands, even her teeth.

As the other woman holds me in her arms, kissing me fiercely, I feel Fernanda's tongue begin to follow the welts made by the belt. She laps the blood from my thighs like a cat as I crouch over the woman on the floor, passionately returning her kisses. I see Fernanda's hand go to the table and take something from it. Her finger pushes into me. I spasm with pleasure, moving my legs further apart for whatever she has planned for me. Her finger moves and I push against it, feeling a new sensation of pain and pleasure. A second finger joins the first and I begin to rock backward against her hand. Then she pulls them out, heedless of my disappointed cry, and pushes something hard inside me. It fills me, stretching me farther than I thought possible, all thought of anything except taking it all in gone from my mind.

Her finger enters my other opening and I enter a world of pleasure that I never imagined before. My moans and cries are pulled from my throat as I surrender all control to her, my demon lover. She possesses me utterly until I collapse upon the woman under me, whose hands touch and fondle me the whole while. Fernanda's hand roughly catches my hair, bending my head back as her teeth sink into my neck. "Make me yours," I whisper. "You already are," she whispers back as I fall away into unconsciousness.

When I recover my strength some days later, I find that she has booked passage on a ship to Spain for me, as well as providing an armed escort to guard my virtue. She gives me documents authorizing the adoption of my daughter by some relatives of the Viceroy. They will keep her nearby, and I can see her grow up as a relative at least, if not as her mother. I cannot keep her myself because an unmarried lady would not be permitted to keep her child. Still, it is more than I dared hope for. As I stand on the ship's deck feeling the uneasy rocking under my feet, I think back to my parting with Fernanda.

"Will you make me like you when I return?" I ask, filled at once with trepidation and desire.

"Do you want to live forever?" she responds, eyes blazing.

"With you," I answered from my heart.

"Perhaps when you return, el Tigre will require some assistance. We will have to see if you are worthy."

"Let me prove it to you," I whisper, stepping closer.

"When you come back. . . ." her fingers pass gently along my cheek, and she vanishes with a swirl of her cloak, leaving me on the dock where I first came to this land. I have only my thoughts of her to warm my bed on the cold shipboard nights. Those and the two punctures in my neck which stay strangely hot to my touch. . . .

A Moment in Time

Deb Atwood

"These habits of yours have got to stop."

Laurie chuckled at the expression on his brother's face. "Really, Jeffrey? And what habits are those?" Standing slowly, he walked over to the bar in his office and calmly poured himself a brandy from a crystal decanter. He offered the bottle to Jeffrey, who refused with a wave of his hand and an expression of disgust. Laurie's smile widened. "So, what is it that offends you? My habits of drinking and eating something other than blood? I realize I no longer need it for sustenance, but I find it a delicious pleasure, difficult to cure myself of." He sipped at the brandy slowly, savoring the taste. "I find it a pity so few of our kind can still enjoy the lovely tastes of this world."

Across the room Jeffrey Cuthbert scowled at his younger brother. "You know that is not the habit of which I am speaking." Crossing the room, he snatched the glass from Laurie's hand, spilling the contents onto the rug. The wet stain spread across the Oriental design as they both stared down at it.

Slowly Laurie raised his eyes to meet his brother's. A faint hint of anger was banished quickly. "Really?" His voice was deceptively mild. "One could never tell by your actions. Do you realize what it will take to clean that stain?"

"Buy another."

Laurie frowned. "You have never had an appreciation for the finer side of life." He reached for the glass still held loosely in Jeffrey's hand, stopping only when the other man clenched his hand shut, tiny shards of glass joining the stain littering the carpet. Laurie shook his head, refusing to meet his brother's eyes. "Overly dramatic. One might almost think you have been persuaded to take up acting."

"I am not here to speak of myself, but of you, Lawrence." Jeffrey brushed the shards from his hands, the cuts healing quickly as he walked away. Laurie merely poured himself another glass. When Jeffrey turned back, the younger of the brothers was seated again on the sofa, legs crossed, the glass already half-empty and held loosely in one hand.

"Ah yes, concerning my bad habits." Laurie smiled. "And exactly which habits were those?"

"The way you involve yourself with mortals is distasteful."

A single eyebrow rose. "And your habits are not?" It took no more than that hint to remind Jeffrey that Laurie knew all his secrets.

"What I do does not matter!" Jeffrey bellowed, losing his composure momentarily. "London is my city, and I am in control here. You answer to me." He reminded Laurie of a dog defending his territory.

Laurie shrugged. "And you find my involvement with mortals a problem. C'est la vie." He finished the final swallow of his brandy, and stood, walking over to open the door to his office. He smiled politely at the slim, dark-haired girl in the hallway. Turning back to Jeffrey he saw that his brother had managed to compose himself once more, his expression the usual calm mask. "I believe Karen is waiting for you, brother."

"If I find that you have allowed another mortal to glimpse the truth about our kind, brother," Jeffrey said darkly, "I will be forced to take action, no matter what your connections with the elders of our race. It is I who hold power here, and it is I who decree what is proper behaviour."

"Of course, brother." Laurie bared his teeth in a dark imitation of a pleasant smile. "I'll do whatever you want, whatever you desire. I live to serve you."

Both heard the sarcasm. Both chose to ignore it as Jeffrey left. Laurie shut the door, his lanky body dropping back onto the sofa, head cradled in his hands. "Damn you, Jeffrey," he muttered. "Just because someone decided to make sure we couldn't die doesn't mean we can't care about those who can." It was a longstanding argument between Laurie and his brother. The elder vampire had never understood the ties Laurie felt with his mortal friends, his enjoyment of their lives. Laurie sighed with frustration. He would never endanger his race by allowing a mortal he did not trust to know the truth about himself.

"Are you all right?"

Laurie's head snapped up at the sound of the voice. His assistant stood in the doorway, her hair pulled back in a ponytail. She was still dressed in running clothes, and a light sheen of sweat was visible on her forehead. He had to smile at the worry on her face. "Yes, Melody, I'm fine. Just another argument with Jeffrey."

She came up behind him, her fingers digging soothingly into his taut shoulder muscles. "Over what this time? How you run the school? Or is Eric coming to visit again and Jeffrey can't stand the thought?"

Laurie allowed a shiver to run through his body at the sound of his sire's name. "God forbid Eric drops in again. A century without him would do me just fine." He sighed with pleasure. "Mmm, don't stop."

Melody laughed. "Hedonist. You just keep me around because I give good backrubs."

His head dipped, allowing her better access to his shoulders. "No, I keep you around because you are the most gifted human mage I know in this forsaken land. And despite what Jeffrey thinks, our kind cannot do without humans."

"You argued over me?" Melody stopped in surprise, fingers resting lightly on his shoulders.

Laurie gave her fingers a reassuring squeeze. "Not you in particular. Just my tendency to become . . . involved . . . with humans in general."

She walked around the couch to sit beside him. "He doesn't seem to me like someone who should throw stones."

"He's not," Laurie agreed. "But he has always been the sort to act as if he were always right. Even when we were children." He sighed, then stood. His desk was spread with papers—students' grades, new admissions to his school. He barely looked at them as he began to file them away. "Melody, do you think you can handle things around here on your own for a while?"

"Don't let him scare you off." Melody's green eyes glittered angrily. "You have just as much right to do what you want in London as he does."

"Of course I do," he replied easily, loosening the tie he had worn in honor of the business meeting with his brother. "Which is why I'm going to go on holiday. Right here in town. Nothing serious; just a bit of a fling." He grinned. "I don't give up, Melody. I thought you knew that."

She found herself grinning back. "I didn't think you would. Take your time; I'll keep everything under control."

"Thanks, girl." He dropped a kiss on her forehead and hurried off to pack a few necessary items.

"Can I get you something?"

The girl's dress was cut low, giving Laurie a broad view as she leaned over the table suggestively, her breasts almost brushing his arm. He smiled distractedly, muttering, "Red wine," as he waved her away.

She pouted, straightening up. "Will that be all, sir?"

He glanced up, seeing her smile at him and pose. "The wine will be all," he said firmly. She frowned and walked away, leaving Laurie to survey the club again.

It was a typical club in this new era of darkly Gothic music. Laurie felt this new generation was the most comfortable he had found since his birth time. With his pale skin, long hair, dark clothes, and flowing poet's shirt, he fit in as if he were born to this time instead of centuries before. The music swirled around him, an underlying rhythm almost like a heartbeat seeming to crawl inside his soul. So many people . . . so fragile.

"Here's your wine." The glass was set down with a slight thunk, and the girl waited only long enough to get her pay before hurrying off to a more accommodating customer. Laurie didn't even notice her leave.

He reached into his pocket and withdrew a vial, emptying it into the wine. He swirled it with a finger as the deep red liquid grew cloudy and thick. He sucked the finger clean, watching the dancers speculatively. Spotting his quarry among the throng around the bar, he quickly downed the contents of the glass. He left the empty behind on the table as he walked away, licking his lips clean.

"Would you care to dance?"

The young man looked up, surprise mirrored in his chocolate eyes. Laurie smiled reassuringly, "Of course, if you would prefer not to . . ."

The man smiled then, sliding off the bar stool. "No, actually I'd love to."

"Well then." Laurie held out a hand, clasping the stranger's firmly in his own. He drew him out to the dance floor, already moving to the slow beat of the music.

The young man had dark hair, cut shorter than most of the others in the club, and deep chocolate eyes. Laurie had to smile at his quarry. He slid his hands around the other's back, pulling him closer as they swayed to the beat.

"Isn't this where you deliver a corny line?" the stranger inquired, chuckling. "Or shall I play the dominant and do the honors?"

Laurie frowned, stepping back slightly. "Just because we are both men does not mean we need to play at any roles." Perhaps Laurie had made a mistake. But he had been watching the man for several nights before deciding to approach. He had considered every option, and this seemed to be the correct one. Had he been wrong?

The stranger shook his head, smiling ruefully. "I'm sorry. I'm not very good at this."

Laurie began to move off the dance floor, drawing the other man with him to a table in one corner of the club. "Perhaps we should talk." If he were wrong, it would be better to find out now, rather than later. And only honesty would tell. "Do you drink brandy?" At the stranger's nod,

Laurie caught the waitress and gave her the order, before settling in at the table. "Where should we start?"

Dark eyes blinked once, and then looked away, off to the dance floor. "Maybe we should start with introductions."

"Lawrence Cuthbert. Most people call me Laurie."

The other man smiled. "Ryan James." He looked just a little more comfortable, and Laurie began to relax. He was moving too fast. He hadn't made a mistake, just a miscalculation.

"Tell me a little about yourself," Laurie encouraged.

Ryan shrugged. "There isn't really much to tell. I'm a student at the university. Majoring in biostatistics. It's a good enough field." He seemed to be defending a choice he hadn't made.

"Good enough," Laurie agreed. There was a long silence, as Ryan toyed with his drink. "Can I be honest?" Laurie finally broke the silence. "Would you prefer if I let you alone?"

Ryan glanced up sharply. "No. It isn't that at all." His eyes softened as he looked at Laurie. "Actually, I . . ." He shrugged. "It's just that I had a companion, and he only moved out about a month ago. I guess I'm not as over it as I thought."

"It does take time," Laurie agreed, reaching out to take Ryan's hand. When the other didn't resist, he squeezed gently. "I'm sorry to have moved so fast."

Slowly Ryan's other hand stole up to cover Laurie's. "It's all right. I was just a little scared for a minute there." He stood, still holding Laurie's hand. "Let's try this again. Would you care to dance?"

"I'd love to." Laurie smiled, allowing himself to be led to the dance floor.

As they danced, Ryan relaxed, his body swaying closer to Laurie's until the two relaxed together on the dance floor, moving easily in synch. Laurie ran a hand over Ryan's back, drawing it up over his shoulder, then touching the pulse on his neck. It fluttered quickly under his fingers, as Ryan's head fell to Laurie's shoulder, exposing the neck to his touch.

Laurie licked his lips, trying to hold the hunger at bay. The night was growing late, and the hunger came more from desire than any true need for sustenance. Gently he pressed a kiss against the skin just below the curve of Ryan's jaw, feeling the pulse jump as the other man sighed. Then he drew away. "I think perhaps it is time for me to go," he said softly.

There was a flicker of regret as Ryan said hesitantly, "I don't live in the dorms. I have a private flat now that Evan's left."

Laurie allowed his own regret to reach his eyes. "It's too soon. You need more time." He slid his hand away from Ryan's neck, over his shoulder, down to his hand. With a gentle squeeze, he stepped away. "Perhaps tomorrow evening you'll be here again?"

Ryan relaxed slightly. "Perhaps." There was a teasing glint in his eyes.

"Then perhaps so shall I," Laurie teased in return.

It wasn't until the doorbell rang a second time that Laurie woke. He blinked twice into the darkness, hand swinging out automatically to switch on the light. A glance at the clock confirmed his suspicions . . . daylight still lit the outside world. The sun would be setting soon, but it seemed far too early to him. Grumbling, he threw a robe over his shoulders and stumbled into the living room of the small flat he had rented for his holiday.

He leaned heavily on the intercom button. "Yes?" His voice was still hoarse with sleep.

There was a pause, then the distinctive beep telling him the button downstairs had been pressed in response. "I'm sorry, did I wake you?"

Laurie tried to recognize the voice, but couldn't. Salesman, most likely. "Something like that, yes. Is this important?"

Another pause. "I'm sorry," the voice repeated. "I'll come back later if you'd like."

"No, I'm awake now." Laurie sighed, and slipped his arms into the robe, fastening the belt about his waist. "What are you selling?"

"I'm . . ." This time the pause seemed to go on forever.

"Yes?" Laurie prompted, beginning to grow impatient.

"I'm not selling anything." The words seemed to tumble out in a jumbled heap. "It's Ryan."

Laurie relaxed against the wall, a half-smile lighting his face as his hand reached for the buzzer. "Come on up."

He could hear footsteps moving slowly up the two flights of stairs, then approaching his door. He swung it open before Ryan had a chance to knock, motioning for him to step inside. Once the door had shut behind him, Ryan simply stared quietly at Laurie, taking in the robe, the disheveled hair, and the imprint of the pillow still on his cheek. With all the shades drawn, Laurie stood half in shadow. Ryan shrugged helplessly.

"I really am sorry. Melody warned me that you're not usually up until six o'clock or so, but I got impatient." His voice trailed off toward the end, like a boy caught with his hand in the cookie jar.

Laurie flashed him a reassuring smile, while wondering how Melody had managed to get on a first name basis with his new friend already. "It's quite all right. Why don't you fix yourself something in the kitchen while I go shower?" He pointed in the appropriate direction.

"Would you care for tea?" Ryan called after him.

"Yes, no sugar or cream," Laurie called back, then shut the door to his bedroom. He took the cordless phone into the bathroom with him, and started the water running before dialing.

"Hello?" Melody sounded a bit rushed.

"You've met Ryan," Laurie said flatly. "Not to mention told him where I'm living. Would you care to enlighten me as to how this came about?"

Melody chuckled. "Well, you did tell him your real name. He's a bright boy, and an attractive one at that. He did a little research, found out about the school, and showed up on the doorstep late this morning. When he asked for you, one of the students sent him to me, since you're officially on holiday. He didn't want to say how he had met you, but I figured out enough to realize that you've already fascinated him. Not bad for a few days' work."

Laurie scowled at the phone. "Thank you for your opinion."

"Any time." There was a pause before Melody asked, "You aren't simply using him to pay back Jeffrey, are you?"

"No, I saw him for the first time a while back," Laurie admitted. "I had been thinking about it, and I just needed to get away from things right now, and Ryan seemed like a pleasant way to do it."

"He seems vulnerable."

Laurie remembered the look on Ryan's face when he talked about his last lover. "Yes, he does. But don't get all mothering over him. I'll take care not to hurt him."

"I expect as much from you, but I wanted to check." She hesitated a moment, then added, "Take care of yourself, Laurie."

"I will. And you do the same."

"Of course."

Laurie set the phone down on the sink, then stepped into the shower. He washed quickly, and toweled dry, his long blond hair hanging loose down his back. He threw on a pair of dark gray sweats, then rejoined Ryan in the living room.

"You look much more awake." Ryan's gaze flickered quickly over him.

"I feel it," Laurie admitted. The phone call and shower had given the sun time to set completely, and he felt much more awake. Seeing Ryan sitting there reminded him that a drink would be in order when possible, but now just wouldn't be a good time. And Ryan wouldn't be a good victim.

Yet.

Laurie accepted the cup of tea Ryan offered, and sipped at it slowly, not certain where to start. Ryan perched on the very edge of the sofa where he sat. He held the teacup in one tense hand while the other hand toyed with the handle of the cup. Laurie avoided sitting on the sofa with him, choosing a nearby chair instead. "Now." He smiled pleasantly. "What is it that I can do for you?"

Ryan blushed lightly. "Actually, I don't go to that club very often, but I hoped . . . that is, I wanted to get together with you anyway."

"Do you like the theatre?"

Ryan cocked his head. "Love it. But I don't have a budget that allows me to go."

Laurie picked up the phone, already dialing. "Thankfully, I do. As well as a friend who has been trying for weeks to get me to see her latest show." He paused while the phone rang, then smiled when he heard his friend's voice. "Remember those tickets you keep trying to force on me?" He chuckled at the response. "All right, all right. You're not trying to force them on me. Would you perhaps be able to set me up with two seats for this evening?" His smile grew. "Under my name at the box office? Thank you, I do appreciate it." He set the phone down and took in Ryan's wide-eyed look. "All settled. We've got an hour or so before we should be there, so would you care to go out for a bite first?"

"Love to." The younger man stood and walked over to face Laurie. "I hope you haven't thought I'm being forward about all this."

"Not at all," Laurie assured him. "It rather flatters me. At my age, I'm not used to being chased."

"At your age?" Ryan laughed. "You must be older than you look. If I didn't know about your position at the school, I'd think you were hardly older than myself."

And with many more mistakes like that, I'll not make it to much older, Laurie cautioned himself. "I'll just be a moment while I change." Back in the privacy of his bedroom, he looked in the mirror. Tall and slim, his features were those of a man in his early twenties. But Laurie had already lived for centuries when Ryan was born. He had watched humans live and die, and had even seen other vampires die. He shook his head, partly dried strands of hair flying wildly. It wouldn't do to think of death at a time like this. It would only depress him, and destroy his evening with Ryan. He quickly changed into something more appropriate for an evening at the theatre, dropping the sweats and slipping on black slacks, a ruffled white shirt, and a gray vest. He tied his hair neatly back in a ponytail, and composed his expression. No more thoughts of death, only life.

When he returned to the living room, Ryan was scanning one of the few books Laurie had brought with him to the flat. He set it down. "Ready to go?"

"Yes." Laurie's smile didn't reach his eyes. Memories intruded, despite his resolve, and he found himself thinking of Jim's Aztec features when he glanced at

Ryan's dark eyes. It had been a year since Jim's death in San Francisco. Since Laurie had returned to London afterward. Obviously he hadn't buried the pain far enough.

"Is something the matter?" Ryan paused at the door.

Laurie shook his head. "Nothing. Just a little tired still. Give me a few moments and I'll be wide awake." He ushered Ryan down to the car.

The exchange left a feeling of friction between the two. Ryan was worried he had done something wrong, and Laurie wasn't quite sure how to relax and begin to enjoy the evening again through the memories. But by the time they finished dinner and reached the theatre, running late after slow service in the restaurant, they had both relaxed and begun to enjoy the evening again.

The lights were blinking, signaling the show was about to begin, as Laurie and Ryan slipped into their seats. The opening music stole over them, and Laurie rested his hand on the arm of the chair between them. By the time the first line was spoken, Ryan's hand had covered Laurie's, and the two sat through the show with fingers entwined.

As the lights slowly came up for intermission, Laurie reluctantly disengaged his fingers from Ryan's. "I'm going to get a bit of something from the bar. Would you care for anything?"

"White wine would be nice," Ryan decided. "Thank you."

Different, Laurie decided as he walked away. Ryan was definitely a breath of fresh air for him. He was nothing like the others Laurie had associated with in recent years, either male or female, and for that he was thankful. He wasn't looking for anyone to replace the others. He wasn't sure what he was looking for, but he hoped he had found it in Ryan.

"You do realize, you are doing exactly what Jeffrey did not want you to do."

The voice was slightly breathy and low, and held a hint of steel. Laurie turned to find Karen standing just behind him, elegant in her low-cut navy evening gown. In her heels she stood tall enough to look him in the eyes, and her gaze was calm and even.

"Is my brother here as well?" Laurie inquired mildly.

"Thankfully, no," Karen admitted. "And I'll even offer to keep quiet this once."

"For a price," Laurie muttered.

"It is a simple one," she agreed. "Stop seeing that mortal."

"Can you prove he is mortal?" Laurie knew that with his magics it only took him one look to know a mortal from a vampire, but for Karen it wouldn't be so easy.

"In time, but he would likely be dead by then, and the point would be moot." Karen paused significantly. Her expression was carefully light. "Would it not?"

She truly was his brother's child, her lazy smile mocking him. He could win, he knew, but did he really want Ryan to be the chess piece in a game between himself and his brother? That had never been his intention. An escape, some peace and quiet, and a loss of bitter memories. Why couldn't it be that simple?

"Well?" she prompted.

Laurie's eyes narrowed as he moved up to the bar. He glared at her briefly, then turned to order two glasses of a good white wine. Accepting the glasses, he raised one between himself and Karen. "To my brother. May he never find out about my companion. The war we would have over your mind would be terrible to behold." He took a sip, watching her eyes.

She took a slow, deep breath, only for show. "You may have a point, and you may not. For now I will not tell him. But in time, never fear, he will learn on his own."

"I don't doubt it," Laurie agreed. "But then it will be between him and me. This is an argument that you and Ryan have nothing to do with." He raised a hand to catch her arm, fingernails biting into the soft flesh. "And you should remember that little detail next time you approach me. If you attack those who are in my protection, my brother can afford you little protection from me in return."

Karen's blue eyes darkened. After a moment of locked eyes, she angrily yanked her arm from his grasp. Angry red marks stood out against her white skin, and thin rivulets of blood ran down to her elbow. "Agreed," she hissed. "You may war with your brother all you like. Do not involve me."

"Agreed." Laurie sipped at his wine as she walked away, her back stiff and heels striking the floor sharply. Such a pleasant girl, in some ways, and one of the more skilled actresses he had known. But she deserved his brother, and Jeffrey's straitlaced ways. Her spirit wasn't free enough for independence.

The lights were already flickering when Laurie slipped back into his seat, handing Ryan's glass to him. Neglecting to let go, Laurie held the glass to Ryan's lips, tipping it slightly while the younger man sipped at the wine. "I am sorry to take so long," Laurie whispered. "I met an old acquaintance in the lobby, and the conversation took longer than I would have expected."

"That's quite all right." Ryan licked a stray drop of wine from his lip, extracting the glass from Laurie's fingers, then turning back to face the stage. "I saw an acquaintance of my own."

Laurie watched the other man carefully, following his gaze. Perhaps a few rows down, and several seats off to the left, a stranger turned and glanced in their direction. Brushing his brown locks out of his eyes, the stranger nodded politely, briefly, then turned away. Laurie felt Ryan's body stiffen next to him, and a bite of jealousy shot through him. "Is that him?"

"Who? Him?" Ryan nodded in the direction of the stranger. He blushed slightly. "Actually, yes. That's Evan. I . . . I think I mentioned him to you last evening?"

"Yes, I believe you did." Laurie's voice masked his emotion, sounding dead even to his ears. "Is he with his new companion?"

"He claims it didn't work out." Ryan's voice sounded slightly choked. "He's with his sister tonight."

Laurie sat silently, turning his concentration to the stage before him. The curtain rose and the characters were still there, and just as believable as before, but it seemed something was missing. Technically, it was an excellent production, and Janine was in her element in the starring role. He would have to introduce Ryan to her after the show. Perhaps. . . .

He glanced over to see that Ryan seemed to be having as much difficulty concentrating on the story as himself. "You miss him," he whispered softly, his hand covering Ryan's on the arm of the chair between them.

Ryan shrugged. "I suppose I do." He bit his lip, and glanced again at Evan, whose dark head was bent in conversation with the girl sitting next to him. Ryan's eyes hardened slightly, and his back stiffened. "But it was his decision, and it was probably for the best." His hand turned under Laurie's, ending up palm to palm, fingers entangling together. "After all, if he hadn't walked out on me, I wouldn't be here with you."

The jealousy seemed to subside somewhat, and Laurie took care to squash it completely. He raised Ryan's hand to his lips, gently kissing the fingertips. "I'm sorry to say it, but I'm glad he walked out on you then."

Ryan's eyes shone as he smiled in return. "Then so am I."

Their attention turned back to the stage, the story engaging their interest again. When Laurie glanced back at Evan one last time, the other man was staring back at the two of them, his expression unreadable in the darkness. Smiling to himself, Laurie released Ryan's hand, and dropped his own arm around his companion's shoulders. A gentle tug, and Ryan leaned into him, head dropping onto Laurie's shoulder.

As Laurie watched, Evan turned away again. Laurie relaxed in the comfortable feeling of Ryan nestling against him, and resolved to enjoy the rest of the show.

"You brought me a gift!" The beautiful blond swept Laurie and Ryan into her dressing room, enveloping Laurie in a warm hug. The silk of her dressing gown tickled his face as she drew her hand over his cheek and chin. "How wonderful of you." She then turned her attention to Ryan, grasping his shoulder firmly, and surveying his face and build. "An attractive one as well. Is he mine to keep?"

Ryan paled, and Laurie bit back his laughter. "No, Janine, he is my companion for the evening. I knew you would never forgive me for seeing your show without stopping backstage, so I persuaded Ryan to accompany me." Stepping forward, he gently disengaged her fingers from Ryan's shoulders, and pulled him back, sliding one hand down to catch Ryan's fingers with his own.

Janine pouted. "You are no fun, Laurie. You never were."

Laurie's smile was fond with remembrance. "Then your memory is failing, my lady."

Her momentary lapse was replaced with a sunny smile. "You are quite right, Laurie. You can be more than fun when you want to be." Her attention snapped back to Ryan. "Keep him, child. He will amuse you and enjoy you."

Ryan's face flooded with color. "I . . ."

"Don't listen to her," Laurie whispered, barely loud enough for Ryan to hear, the warm breath softly tickling his ear. "Janine has always run off at the mouth when she shouldn't. Just pay her no mind, and you'll be happier."

"Are you going to introduce me properly?" Janine asked cheerfully, as if she had no idea what Laurie had just said; both knew that she had heard it perfectly well.

"Janine Sanders, please meet Ryan James." Laurie gave Ryan's hand a gentle squeeze. "Ryan, Janine is one of the foremost actresses of the era."

"Your show was wonderful," Ryan enthused, beginning to relax.

"Really?" Janine had never been one to resist praise. "So tell me," she motioned to a couch, and both settled down, "what did you think of the staging in the scene where . . ."

Laurie stepped away as the two dropped into an enthusiastic discussion of the production. While Ryan obviously had no background in the theatre, he knew what he enjoyed seeing, and had very definite opinions. And Janine, of course, loved to play to an audience, and Ryan was momentarily captive.

After more than an hour, Ryan glanced over to where Laurie stood, a half-smile on his face as he watched the pair chatter. Laurie's smile broadened at the look of dismay on Ryan's face. "I'm so sorry. I believe I was distracted."

"Janine will do that to anybody," Laurie assured him. "If I hadn't expected to spend quite a bit of time backstage, I never would have brought you here."

"It has been a lovely visit." Janine languidly rose from the couch, one arm outstretched to Ryan. He helped her to her feet, gently kissing the back of her hand. "Please, do bring your companion again." Her voice was light as she said it, but it held the sound of an order to Laurie's ears.

He cocked his head, eyes narrowing slightly. Following her gaze to Ryan's neck, he shook his head slightly. Janine began to pout, but pushed Ryan toward Laurie. Ryan, oblivious to the byplay, merely walked over to stand by the door. "I'd love to come by again, sometime, Janine, if you wouldn't mind."

"As soon as we get the chance." Laurie ushered Ryan out the door before Janine could protest.

"You sound upset."

Laurie's eyes widened, surprised that Ryan had caught that. Then he frowned to realize the jealousy that must have displayed so briefly on his face and in his voice. "She would eat you alive," he muttered.

"I doubt that." Ryan laughed.

"You'd be surprised." Laurie's voice was too low for Ryan to hear. "Would you prefer me to admit that I'm jealous?"

Ryan stopped walking, turning to face Laurie. "Are you really? Why?"

Laurie shrugged, and simply drew Ryan toward him, kissing him gently. He stepped back, trying to measure the bewildered expression in Ryan's eyes. *So young, so alive.* There was a hint of bitterness as Laurie said, "I'm not sure why I'm jealous. But I am."

Ryan turned away, and began walking again. He was silent until they reached the car, and Laurie began to drive away. When he finally spoke, his voice was low. "Have you slept with her?"

"Janine?"

Ryan nodded. "She seemed . . . familiar."

"We've known each other a long time." Laurie's fingers tightened on the steering wheel slightly, thinking just how long that time was. "And yes, long ago in our past, we were rather intimate."

Ryan was staring out the window, the back of his head to Laurie, gazing into the darkness. "It couldn't be that long ago."

"Long enough." Laurie tried to put an end to the queries with a note of finality. It worked, and the silence grew uncomfortable.

Laurie reached out, fingers falling softly on Ryan's shoulder, until the younger man turned to face front once more. Laurie let his hand fall down over his shoulder, clasping Ryan's hand in his own. No response. Laurie's hand fell to the seat between them, and he started drum his fingers against the leather seat.

"I don't know how you do it."

"Do what?" Laurie kept his voice casual, wishing he dared look inside Ryan's mind, but hating the idea of invading his privacy that way.

"I think I'm jealous," Ryan admitted. "I keep thinking of you and Janine, and wondering . . . why did you stop seeing her? How can you be such good friends now? I don't think I could ever be friends with Evan again. And. . . ." his voice trailed off, and there seemed to be a small catch in his throat. "If you had a relationship with her, a normal relationship, whyever would you want one with me?"

Laurie's hands clenched in surprise. He couldn't keep the anger from his voice. "What the bloody hell do you mean by that?"

Ryan shrugged, turning to look back out the window again. "If you sleep with women, if you can sleep with women . . . I just don't understand what you want with me."

Laurie jerked the steering wheel hard, stomping on the brakes to skid to a stop at the side of the road. Luckily, at that late hour, it was nearly deserted, and the one lone car behind them swung around easily. He gave himself a few seconds to calm down. "What, exactly, is it that you are trying to say, Ryan?"

Ryan swallowed hard. "Do you have to make this so difficult? You know what I'm like, what my preferences are. I thought . . ." he blushed, barely visible in the darkness. "I thought you were the same. But I guess you're not."

"Are you saying that because I have, in the past, had a relationship with a woman, that I'm not good enough for you?" Laurie's voice was dangerously low.

"No!" Ryan's voice echoed in the confines of the car as he shouted his surprise. "It's just that a man wanting a woman is normal . . ."

"Are you trying to say that my wanting you is not normal?"

"It's perfectly normal, for me," Ryan allowed, "but not for you."

"Oh, bloody hell," Laurie swore. "Look, Ryan, there are a lot of things you don't know about me, that you may never know about me, and that you may not understand." Running his fingers through his hair in frustration, his fingers caught in the ribbon holding his ponytail and he yanked it out. Long blond strands framed his face, slightly tangled from the ribbon having been removed. "Ryan, my relationship with Janine, or with anyone else in my past, has nothing to do with might happen between us. Nothing."

Ryan's chocolate eyes reflected in the lights of a passing driver, and Laurie read confusion, insecurity, and a glimmer of hope. He sighed, deciding to forget talking about it. Reaching out, he clasped Ryan's shoulders and pulled him close, kissing him gently. "There," he said softly, "does that make my point?"

Ryan sat back slightly, a quirk of a smile barely beginning. "I think so. Care to reinforce it?"

And Laurie did.

"Would you like to do something this evening?"

Laurie yawned, hiding the soft sound from the phone. Even after two weeks, Ryan still called him before sundown. Someday, perhaps, he'd change, but Laurie enjoyed his enthusiasm, and his company. "Did you have something in particular in mind?"

"Well," Ryan hesitated. "We've done something just about every night, going to the club, and the theatre, and . . ."

Laurie frowned. Ryan's insecurity must be wearing off on him, he decided, as he asked, "Have we been spending too much time together?"

"Not at all!" Ryan insisted. Laurie could almost picture him grinning on the other end of the phone. "I was just thinking that perhaps it might be nice to have a quieter evening. I could pick up some fish and chips on my way over, and a bottle of good rosé. What do you say?"

"Sounds wonderful," Laurie agreed. "Give me a half hour to crawl out of bed." He was still smiling at the click of the phone, then yawned again. Slowly he climbed out of bed, forcing himself to stay awake. It wasn't long until dark, but it was hard to stay awake during even the shortest of daylight hours. A slowly warming shower helped, as well as the eventual setting of the sun.

He dressed carefully, but casually. Gray slacks, a black T-shirt. He didn't bother to dry his hair, simply tugging it back with a leather strip. No socks or shoes either. He always preferred his freedom, and if they weren't going out, there was no need for formality.

When the doorbell rang, he hurried to get the buzzer. Ryan's footsteps moved slowly up the stairs, and Laurie had the door open to greet him. At the sight of Ryan, Laurie forgot what he had planned to say. "Hi."

"Hi yourself." Ryan stopped a short way from Laurie, smiling shyly. "Well?" Holding out a bottle in a bag, he added softly, "Here."

Laurie stepped back from the door, motioning for Ryan to step in as he took the bottle from him. "Not bad," he decided, scanning the label quickly.

"I've got dinner as well," Ryan reminded him.

"Wonderful." Laurie watched as Ryan moved to the table and began to lay out the meal. Ryan was comfortable in Laurie's flat already, finding the plates and silverware easily. "Wineglasses are above the sink," Laurie offered, when Ryan faltered.

"Thanks." Ryan walked back, slipping the bottle from Laurie's hand. "Would you care to join me?" He filled both glasses, then handed one to Laurie. "You're being terribly quiet. Is something the matter?"

Laurie shook himself slightly. "No, no, nothing." He forced a smile to his face, trying to shake the nervousness he felt. Ryan was one more man, one more relationship. One more meal. After centuries, that was the only sane way to see it.

Ryan raised his glass. "To two weeks."

"Two weeks, and more," Laurie agreed. Stepping forward, he took the glass from Ryan, kissing him quickly. "Let's get to dinner before it gets cold." He smiled softly. "It's always best to eat a meal hot."

Both were silent during the meal, Laurie reflecting on his plans for the evening, and Ryan silently observing. Once everything was finished, the table cleaned, and the dishes taken care of, Laurie felt a familiar hunger and an equally unfamiliar set of nerves fall over him. "Perhaps you'd care to watch the telly?"

Ryan shrugged. "It's up to you. To be perfectly honest, I just couldn't stand the thought of spending another evening wearing something dressy and uncomfortable." He gestured at his jeans and T-shirt. "As much as I've enjoyed the theatre and shows and dinners, I'd much rather just spend time with you." He blushed slightly.

Laurie began to relax. "Then perhaps a show or two." Snagging the remains of the wine, and the glasses, he led the way into the living room.

Reclining on the couch, Laurie draped an arm about Ryan's shoulder, enjoying the feel of the younger man cradled against his side. As a comedy droned on across the room, Laurie ignored it, gently stroking Ryan's neck, feeling the pulse jump under his fingers.

"Much better," Ryan whispered. His hand had settled on Laurie's knee, and stayed there, fingers splayed over the leg. "Don't stop." He sounded surprised when Laurie's fingers left his neck.

Laurie chuckled. "Don't tell me you have a sensitive neck." He could feel the heat rising under his fingertips as Ryan blushed.

"Hell, yes."

"That could make the evening very interesting. You might say I have a fondness for necks myself." Laurie sat up, turning to face Ryan. He took the younger man's chin in his hand, tipping his head back. "Now, where is best to start?" he mused.

Laurie began to nibble just below Ryan's ear. He worked his way down, licking at the side of the neck, arriving finally at the crest of the collarbone. Ryan sighed, his head dropping back, exposing more of the tender flesh. Laurie drew back, and held his breath, bringing the sudden hunger back under control.

Ryan's eyes flickered open, and he pulled himself forward to glare at Laurie. "Don't you dare stop again," he ordered. There was a sudden confidence in his voice as he pulled Laurie forward, kissing him firmly. "You started this," Ryan muttered against his lips, "and we're going to finish it."

Laurie smiled. "Damn straight." And then he bent back to what he had been doing. He could feel the hunger still, but something else interfered. No matter how strong the thirst was, the desire was stronger. As Ryan's hands gently, then roughly, caressed his body he realized that Ryan was far more than another simple mortal.

Laurie worked slowly, unbuttoning Ryan's shirt a single button at a time, trailing his fingernail across Ryan's chest. He untucked the tails of the shirt from Ryan's jeans and then slid it over his shoulders. He then moved slightly so that he sat behind Ryan on the couch, and nibbled on the back of his neck. Ryan swayed back, leaning against him, one hand stroking Laurie's leg.

"I like it," Ryan murmured.

"That's the point," Laurie chuckled. He reached around and unzipped Ryan's jeans, one hand sliding inside slowly. The muscles under the skin jumped as Laurie's hand slid over Ryan's stomach, then he sighed deeply as Laurie's pale fingers curled around the darker length of Ryan's cock. "And let me guess, you like that as well," Laurie whispered.

Ryan didn't bother to answer out loud, stretching back to allow Laurie easier access to his body. His hips began to move gently against Laurie's questing hand, until the vampire laughed. "Not yet, luv." He pushed Ryan away. "Stand up, and finish getting yourself undressed."

He enjoyed the show as Ryan slid his jeans over slim hips, his briefs following them quickly as he kicked them across the room. Shoes, then socks, then Ryan stood there, hands on his hips, glaring playfully at his lover. "Seems a bit unfair," he grinned. "Me standing here in the buff and all, while you're still dressed."

Laurie stretched languidly along the couch, hands behind his head. "So do something about it."

"With pleasure." Ryan tugged the T-shirt over Laurie's head, throwing it off to one side. Then he knelt on the floor and carefully touched the bulge under Laurie's slacks. With one hand, Ryan reached to loosen the zipper, his other hand caressing Laurie through the strained fabric. Laurie raised his hips, allowed Ryan to slip the slacks over them. His cock made a tent in his boxers, and Ryan smiled as he slipped those away as well. "Much better," he whispered, lowering his lips to engulf Laurie's hard length.

"Oh. . . ."

Ryan's tongue swirled around the tip of Laurie's cock, tasting it gently, then he roughly engulfed it, pulling hard. All the while one hand dipped below to cradle and stroke his balls. Laurie groaned as Ryan bent before him, tongue working magically over him. The vampire's fingers tangled in Ryan's short chocolate locks, begging him not to leave, until with a final moan Laurie pushed him away.

"Not yet." His voice was hoarse as he motioned for Ryan to join him again on the couch. "Here, sit on my lap."

Ryan raised an eyebrow, curiously, but did as he said, settling back against him. He could feel the hard length nestled between his cheeks, and he rocked back slightly against it, until Laurie's hands on his hips stilled him.

"If you keep that up," Laurie whispered, "I am going to lose control. And I don't want to lose control"—He paused significantly—"yet." His hand dropped back to stroke Ryan again, while he claimed the younger man's lips with his own.

"Please, Laurie," Ryan whispered. His lover didn't have to ask what for, stroking him. Ryan was breathing hard as Laurie pulled him up, moving so that Ryan was kneeling on the couch.

"Stay right there," Laurie whispered. He held one hand out to the side, and in a flash of magic a small foil packet appeared between his fingers. He tore the wrapper, quickly sliding the condom over his erection. He stroked along it, taking the lubricant to smooth into the crack of Ryan's ass.

Laurie knelt on the couch behind Ryan. Positioning himself carefully, he slid into the other man's ass. Both men groaned with the sensation.

"Lean back," Laurie ordered softly. Somehow they managed it, maneuvering carefully until Laurie sat again on the couch, and Ryan was on his lap, with Laurie still buried inside of him. Laurie's hips began to rock slowly, as his hand echoed the motion on Ryan's cock.

"Now, Laurie," Ryan urged. "Please!" He was breathing in short gasps, his head falling back against Laurie's shoulder, baring his throat. His hips bucked forward, clenching around Laurie's length even as Ryan thrust his own cock against the vampire's hand.

Laurie set his lips against the soft skin of Ryan's neck, feeling the pulse fluttering there. Ryan sighed, his eyes closed in passion. Laurie couldn't restrain himself any longer, neither his hunger for Ryan's body or for his blood. As his teeth slipped into the vein, he could feel Ryan's body shudder against him as Laurie's own tremors began.

Laurie gently licked Ryan's neck, feeling the wounds close beneath his tongue. Slight tremors still shook his mortal body, and Laurie simply held him, waiting for the tremors to die down.

The sounds of the telly still sounded across the room; one show ended and another began before Ryan stirred and sat up. He disengaged himself and began to move around the room, silently picking up discarded clothing, sorting out the items.

"Going somewhere?" Laurie asked mildly.

Ryan glanced over in surprise. "It's gotten pretty late. You usually kick me out right about now."

Laurie stretched lazily along the couch, drawing Ryan's attention easily to him. He smiled and licked his lips. "What if I asked you to stay tonight."

"I'd ask if you're sure," Ryan told him, his chocolate eyes serious.

"Dead serious," Laurie assured him. "Do you have anything to do tomorrow? I'd love to keep you to myself tonight."

A slow smile began to spread across Ryan's face, the light reaching his eyes quickly. "And I'd love to stay."

Laurie stood, taking the shirt from Ryan's hand, dropping it back on the floor. Taking his hand, he drew him towards the bedroom in the back of the flat. "There's only one condition to this," he cautioned. "Don't you dare wake me up during the day tomorrow."

"Agreed."

Laurie laughed at the answer. Thankfully, all the windows were magically barred. He doubted Ryan would ever keep that promise. And he didn't care. He'd taken care of his thirst. Now he wanted to spend the rest of the night enjoying his time with Ryan.

"I'm in love." Laurie's voice fell flat into the silence.

"You don't sound happy about it," Melody commented drily as she looked up from her stack of paperwork. Catching sight of the expression on his face, her eyes widened slightly. "Oh my, you don't look happy either."

"I'm happy," Laurie muttered, dropping his lanky frame onto the couch in his office. "And I'm not happy." He ran his fingers through his hair, drawing the long strands back, then dropping them so that they hung over his face. "Dammit, I just wasn't expecting to fall in love."

Melody walked over to the couch, settling carefully next to him. "I take it this is that fellow who stopped by a few weeks ago?"

"Ryan, yes," Laurie agreed. "We've gotten quite close since then." He leaned forward, chin on his hands. "The thing is, Melody, Ryan's mortal. Therefore, he's dinner. And that's all he should be to me." Leaning back again, he sighed dramatically. "A damnably attractive goblet of blood."

Melody chuckled. "I'm mortal. Am I just dinner?"

"While I have nibbled on your neck on occasion," Laurie told her, "you're not just dinner to me. But I wouldn't say I'm in love with you, either."

Melody considered him as he sprawled across the couch. His face was paler than usual, and his clothes were wrinkled. The shirt looked slept in, and his eyes were drawn together in a deep frown. It almost looked as if he had worry lines by his eyes. "This is really bothering you, isn't it? You really are upset that you're in love with him." She covered his hand with her own, squeezing gently. "Why is it so bad?"

"He's mortal, dammit!" Laurie jumped up and stalked away, pacing around the room. He gestured broadly as his voice rose in his agitation. "Vampires can't fall in love with mortals. It just doesn't happen. It isn't worth anything. Mortals die."

Melody didn't try to hide a wry smile. "And vampires don't."

Laurie crumpled, as if he'd been struck, ending up semi-seated on the floor. "No, you're quite right. Vampires most certainly do die. And almost as unexpectedly as mortals do."

The thought seemed to hang in the air between them. Laurie had been despondent when he returned from the States nearly a year before. His relationship with Jim had still been new when the Aztec vampire had died in a firebombing. It had been months before Laurie could stop his frenzied work long enough to confide in his partner.

"I'm sorry."

Laurie sighed. "I deserved it. You are right. I shouldn't hold it against him that he's mortal."

"You don't seem any happier," Melody observed.

"No," he sighed again, "I'm not. I'm almost beginning to wonder if Jeffrey is right. Maybe I should stop involving myself with mortals."

"Close the school? Abandon me?" Melody teased.

"I already told you, you're different. You don't count as a mortal."

"I'd love it if you'd remind the deities in power of that when it comes time for me to die," Melody quipped.

Laurie forced a smile. "I could fix that mortality problem of yours in an instant."

"You could do the same for Ryan if you wanted, as well."

"If he wanted," Laurie looked away. He walked over to the window, and stared out into the cool night. "I've never discussed it with him. It just hasn't come up."

"You haven't . . ."

"I've tasted his blood, yes," Laurie answered her unasked question. "But we haven't talked about it. He hasn't asked any questions, and I haven't felt like volunteering."

"How long?"

Laurie shrugged. "A week. It's . . ." He drew a deep breath, filling his lungs slowly, feeling the pressure of the air inside. He didn't need to breathe, but it still helped calm him, letting the air out little by little while he tried to put his thoughts together. "I can't resist him. I barely tasted him, and he is so . . . his neck is so sensitive, he's so responsive. The reaction he has to everything is part of what I love about him. I want to keep giving him that joy."

"So do it."

"How?" He felt helpless, confused. Melody suddenly sounded far older than him. "I don't know how to do it, without changing him somehow. I have to explain everything to him, and I'm afraid it will make a difference." His fingers tightened on the windowsill, nails digging tiny half moons into the wood. "I've never actually had a relationship with someone who didn't know who I was, or what I was, before it began."

"Does he love you?"

Laurie shook his head. "I don't know."

Melody approached to stand behind him, hands on his shoulders, rubbing gently. "Have you told him you love him?"

Laurie's head dropped forward, hair shadowing his face. "No."

"Then what do you think your next step is?"

Laurie straightened, shrugging her touch off. "You really believe in honesty, don't you?"

"Lying is making you miserable," Melody confirmed. "I'd rather have you sitting here telling me you love him and being happy about it, instead of worrying about what he's going to do when you tell him you're an evil creature of the night. So just go and do it."

Laurie walked over to the desk and yanked a drawer open, pulling out a brush. He tugged it through the tangled strands of his hair, grunting with the pain as it resisted being brushed. Finally the long locks hung straight around his face, and he dropped the brush back into the drawer, drawing out an elastic instead. He quickly braided his hair, and twisted the elastic firmly around the end. A single strand escaped, falling across his nose when he turned back to look at Melody.

"Fine, I'll do it your way." His back was stiff and resolute as he turned to leave. "You're right. Whether he rejects me, or agrees with me, or. . . ." Watching, Melody saw his shoulders suddenly slump, then Laurie turned to face her again. "Whatever he says, you'll still listen to me, right? Even if I did say you didn't count."

"I'll still listen to you." Melody smiled encouragingly. She had never seen Laurie this nervous, this insecure. "That's what friends are for, to pick up the pieces."

Laurie clasped her hands, squeezing tightly them tightly, then releasing her. "Thanks. Wish me luck."

"Good luck." Melody smiled at the closing door. "But I doubt you'll need it."

Laurie hit the buzzer to let his guest in. Whistling, he strode to the door, and whipped it open. Footsteps were still coming up the stairs. "Hello, Ryan," he called out cheerfully.

"Is that his name?" Jeffrey's voice was dry and his expression sour as he came into view. "I take it you are expecting his company this evening."

"As a matter of fact, I am." Laurie turned on his heel and walked away, leaving Jeffrey in the doorway. "Come

in," he called back, "and shut the door behind you. Both
of you."

Jeffrey stepped inside, and motioned for Karen to
follow. As he removed his gloves, Jeffrey surveyed the flat,
while Karen hovered near the door.

"You don't have to be on guard duty," Laurie told her.
"No one is going to be attacking you here. Ryan isn't a
hunter."

"You trust mortals too easily," Jeffrey reminded him.
"What evidence do you have that he can be trusted?"

"None at all, without going into his mind." Laurie's
eyes hardened suddenly. "And don't order me to do that,
Jeffrey. Because I won't. I do trust Ryan, and that is
something you will have to learn to understand."

A hint of bitterness crossed his face as he turned to
Karen. "As for yourself, I thought you had made me a
promise."

She lowered her eyes. "I had agreed not to tell Jeffrey,
that is true." Laurie saw the flash of anger in his brother's
eyes, but Karen carefully did not look at either of the men.
"But I also agreed that while I would not aid him, neither
would I hinder him."

"You are a vampire," Jeffrey reminded him. "And he is
human. He is cattle, good only for manipulation or
dinner."

Laurie raised an eyebrow, a bit of humor returning.
"Oh? And what would you do during the day without
your human servants? Do you trust them?"

"I control them."

Laurie shuddered delicately at Jeffrey's statement. "You
would have done well in the feudal age, brother. What a
pity you can't return London to that time." He walked
away, and busied his hands arranging a setting for two on
the table. "But whether you control the mortals who
protect you during the day or not, the fact remains, you

cannot control me. And as I am my sire's child, I doubt you wish to cross me, either." While Laurie had never liked his sire, he recognized the use of Eric's standing within their race. "I will take any action against Ryan as a direct action against myself." Laurie's expression was mild as he turned to face Jeffrey once more. "Is that clear?"

"And should you reveal yourself to that mortal, I will accept that you have endangered all our kind and deal with you accordingly." Jeffrey's voice was deep and solemn. "I believe our elders will agree with any action I might take."

Eyes locked, neither would look away. "My sire might have something different to say," Laurie said simply. He held his brother's gaze a moment longer before purposefully turning his back. "May I get you something?"

He heard a small sound, as if Karen began to speak, but Jeffrey interrupted. "No, we will be leaving soon."

"Not soon enough," Laurie muttered. He didn't care if he was overheard; Jeffrey already knew his opinion.

When the bell to the flat rang, Karen reached the door before Laurie could, swinging it wide.

Ryan stopped in the doorway, looking curiously into the apartment. "Am I interrupting something?"

Laurie sighed. "No, come on in. I've got everything set up for dinner, if you don't mind eating in."

"Not at all." Ryan stepped in, and watched as Karen closed the door behind him. She merely watched him in return, a slight smile on her face. Looking away, Ryan stepped close to Laurie. "Are you certain I'm not interrupting? I can always stop back later." He chuckled softly. "And after I was so careful not to call and wake you up this evening, too."

Laurie stifled a groan at the frown on Jeffrey's face at the last comment. "They were on their way out anyway." He motioned toward the couch. "This is my brother Jeffrey, and the lovely young lady at the door is his companion Karen." Laurie slid an arm around Ryan's waist, tugging him gently closer. "Brother, this is Ryan." Laurie smiled at his companion, then kissed him, deepening the kiss as Ryan responded.

Ryan drew back after a moment. "If we start now, we'll never have dinner," he reminded Laurie. After a glance at Jeffrey, he added, "And I don't think your brother approves."

Laurie hid a smile at his brother's glowering expression. "My brother has never approved of my lifestyle," he agreed. "And he likely never will. He will simply have to learn to agree to disagree."

Jeffrey stood, tugging black gloves over his hands. "Perhaps," he acknowledged. "But that is something we can discuss later. For now, you would do well to remember what we have already discussed this evening."

"As would you," Laurie agreed. He watched as the door swung shut behind the other two, then slowly dropped his strong hold on Ryan. "As would you," he repeated softly.

"I'm not causing you any family problems, am I?" Ryan's chocolate eyes mirrored his concern. "I'd hate to think I'm coming between you and your family."

"You would not be the first thing to come between us." Laurie sighed. "My relationship with my brother has never been a good one, and the years have only made it worse." He flashed a bright smile and drew Ryan to him. "But that has little to do with tonight. Did you have any plans for the evening?"

Ryan laughed and grinned, eyes dark with desire. "Dinner, and maybe dessert." He frowned as Laurie abruptly pulled away from him, turning his back. "What's wrong?"

Laurie kept his back to him, tongue running over his sharp canines. It took a minute before he was under control again. "Nothing." He managed to keep his voice from shaking. "The argument with Jeffrey must have bothered me more than I thought."

"Are you certain you want company this evening?"

Laurie didn't say a word, merely walking into the kitchen and returning with a tray. "And let my home-cooked meal go to waste? I hardly ever cook, so you must at least try it." His grin showed his return to good humor. "After all, I may not cook like this again for years."

"It looks wonderful." Ryan took the plate of fettucini from the tray and set it on the table. Moments later they were seated, and Ryan made a noise deep in his throat as he tasted the meal. "This is wonderful. What do you mean you won't cook again for years?"

It would be the perfect moment. Laurie slowly chewed, swallowed, and tried to work up the nerve to say it. Then a sip of wine. When he looked at Ryan, he was waiting patiently for an answer. "It's an exaggeration." Laurie sighed, mentally cursing himself. "I'm an excellent cook, but I so rarely do it. My friends say it's like I cook only once every decade." *Which is true*, he admitted to himself.

Ryan accepted the answer, silently finishing dinner. "I hope I'm around the next time you decide to cook, then." He flashed a quick grin, then disappeared into the kitchen with the dirty dishes.

Something turned over in Laurie's stomach. Next time . . . he liked the idea. Standing, he shook his head. Melody was right. He had to talk to Ryan, and soon.

"Where are you wandering off to?" He hadn't even heard Ryan come up behind him. The other man slipped his arms around Laurie's waist. "You look like you're a million miles from here."

"Just thinking of you." Laurie sighed as one of Ryan's hands caressed his chest. He could feel Ryan's body against the length of his back, cheek pressed into Laurie's shoulder. "Where do you want me to be?"

"Here," Ryan whispered. "In my arms. Now." He groaned softly. "Please?" He easily untucked Laurie's shirt, pulling so that Laurie had to lift his arms and allow it to slide over his head. Then Ryan's hands sought the zipper. . . .

Laurie turned in his arms, forgetting everything else. "Damn." He kissed Ryan, nibbling on his lower lip and caressing his ass until Ryan began to moan. The fair-haired vampire stepped back long enough to allow both to shed their clothes quickly, then their bodies entwined again.

"Please?" Ryan's voice was choked, barely a whisper.

"No." Laurie slowly pushed Ryan down to the floor, covering his body with his own. "Not yet."

Skillfully he stroked Ryan's body to the breaking point, not allowing him his release. He ran one fingernail across the sensitive balls as his teeth nibbled gently at Ryan's cock. He began to slide his mouth along Ryan's hardened length, sliding it in and out as his tongue swirled over the knob at the end. He flicked his tongue, tasting the salty drop from the tip, then drew back slightly. He moved down to Ryan's knees, kissing the backs gently. Ryan moaned as Laurie's lips and tongue traveled upward, swirling little whirlpools of sensation across the other man's thighs.

"Please. . . ." Ryan moaned.

Laurie didn't answer, allowing his tongue to come close to Ryan's balls, then close to his cock, but not reaching them. His hands were clasped with Ryan's, holding both out to the side. Nothing touched Ryan where he desperately desired it. Nothing. Ryan's hips thrust ineffectually against the air.

"Goddammit, Laurie, please!" Ryan groaned. Laurie obliged then, taking one of Ryan's balls into his mouth, rolling it around, then slipping it back out so he could take the other one. Then he moved back up to the cock that had stroked his cheek as he caressed the balls with his tongue.

Ryan was whimpering, alternately pleading and damning Laurie with every breath. The vampire moved up over him, planting his knees on either side of Ryan's head as he lay back on the rug. "Take it," Laurie ordered, and Ryan did, reaching up and drawing Laurie's hardness into his mouth. He sucked frantically, begging for more, as Laurie reached back behind him, continuing to stroke.

Laurie felt his balls tighten, and he jerked back roughly. Ryan groaned, and reached for him, but Laurie slipped quickly away to lie next to him. He felt Ryan's hands curl around him, stroking and pulling, as he did the same to him. Laurie moved up over his lover, dropping light kisses on his lips, across his cheek, then down to his neck. And when Ryan could only whimper incoherently, Laurie finally gave in, sinking his teeth into the vein as they both slipped over the edge.

Laurie lay half on top of Ryan, his head cradled against Ryan's shoulder, one leg and one arm splayed over the other man's body. With one hand, Ryan gently stroked Laurie's hair.

"I wish it could be like this forever."

Laurie suppressed a shiver. "Just like this?" He chuckled. "Do you want to live forever?"

Ryan was silent a moment. Then he sighed. "It's a nice dream, isn't it? Never dying, I mean. Never having to grow old and die."

Laurie slipped away and propped himself up on one elbow. "What if it were possible, I mean. Would you want to live forever?"

"It's impossible." Ryan discounted the idea.

"But what if, Ryan?" Laurie smiled, and poked him in the ribs, getting a laugh in response as Ryan tried to move away from the tickling. "Play the game. What if it were possible to live forever? Would you?"

Ryan locked his hands under his head, elbows out, staring up at the ceiling. "Is there a price?"

Laurie shrugged. "There are a lot of different ways to be immortal. According to fiction anyway." He took a deep breath. "What if you were a vampire?"

"A vampire?" Ryan sat up suddenly, laughing. "You mean the kind of chap who runs around in a cape saying, 'I vant to suck your blood'?"

"Well, the bloodsucking type anyway." Laurie frowned as Ryan started to laugh again. "You're not playing the game, Ryan."

"All right, all right." Ryan swallowed and managed to stop laughing. "I'll try to take you seriously." He sat and thought, chewing on his lip. Laurie watched him, catching his eye long enough to catch fleeting thoughts and emotions.

"I. . . ." Ryan hesitated.

Laurie felt a sudden fleeting moment of horror from Ryan.

"Would I have to kill?" His voice dropped to a whisper.

Laurie shook his head. "No killing. Just small sips of blood." He licked his lips unconsciously. "Your victim probably wouldn't even notice."

Ryan was silent for long enough that Laurie wished he dared peer inside his mind to see what he was thinking about.

"I don't think I'd like it."

Laurie hid his disappointment. "Why not?"

"I'd hate to see everyone I know die. I'd hate hurting people just so that I could live."

"What if it didn't hurt them?"

Ryan rolled over, his back to Laurie, curled up in a ball. "It wouldn't matter if it hurt them or not. I'd still be robbing them of something they couldn't live without, just to sustain my own life. It wouldn't be right."

Laurie stroked his back, his expression sad. "It's only make believe, Ryan." He tugged on his shoulder until Ryan turned to face him again. He smiled reassuringly. "Vampires aren't real."

"I know," Ryan admitted. "All those thoughts of losing people, and dying, and killing . . . it gets to me."

"Don't." Laurie shushed him with a kiss. "Don't even think about it. This is life." He allowed his hands to wander across his lover's body, bringing Ryan quickly out of his depression.

This time when he drew out the lovemaking it was slow and languid, no hurry, no fever pitch. A strong reaffirmation of life and the living.

"Maybe not forever," Ryan whispered when it was over. He didn't try to suppress his yawn, curling his sated body into Laurie's.

Laurie sat up, his hand still stroking Ryan's side. In moments Ryan was asleep. With a little effort Laurie slipped inside his mind to read a few residual thoughts. Ryan was horrified at the idea of vampirism, at the idea of what Laurie did.

"I love you." Laurie brushed away the tear that fell onto Ryan's back. With another few moment's effort the vampire was inside Ryan's mind completely. Everything was laid bare before him. He didn't look, couldn't look. Didn't want to know how Ryan really felt about him. It didn't matter anymore.

Ryan would never understand who Laurie was. He couldn't tell him; he couldn't not tell him. If he kept him, Jeffrey would use him. Laurie shivered at the image of Jeffrey with his lips at Ryan's neck.

It would be better this way. Better to end it now, before the caring got to be too much. Better to let go.

Laurie sat at the desk, a mound of paperwork before him, the pen dangling between his fingertips. Melody hadn't bothered to knock before walking into his study, and he hadn't even noticed her arrive. She stood there, watching him as the cap of the pen slipped between his teeth and he gently chewed on the tip, brows furrowed in concentration.

"Hard at work?" she broke the silence.

His head snapped up. "What in bloody hell are you doing here?"

"Checking up on you," she admitted. "You've been a bear the last few days. Last I knew you were in love. Want to talk about it?"

Laurie leaned back, placing the pen between his teeth again. Seconds later he yanked it from between his lips and slammed it down on the desk, glaring at it. "I think I need a drink," he muttered. "Want to go with me?"

Melody looked him over. Physically he looked fine. Better, in fact, than he had since coming back from the States a year ago. But his eyes were shadowed. "Let me get my coat." She stood, then paused. "We are talking about alcohol here, right?"

"Just get your coat."

He met her at the door, and walked her silently to the car.

"Where are we going?" She waited for an answer, more concerned when he was silent. His face was unreadable as he drove. "What did Jeffrey have to say yesterday?"

Laurie's back stiffened. "Nothing important." His fingers tightened on the wheel.

It had been a short visit, Karen hovering in the background like a dutiful shadow, while Jeffrey loomed large in Laurie's study. "I see you are back at work." Jeffrey's voice was cool, clipped.

"Yes," Laurie admitted. "Is that good enough for you?"

"Until you step outside the bounds again."

The brothers had stood nose to nose then, and Laurie's eyes darkened with crimson anger. "Leave Ryan alone. He is no longer a part of this."

"Agreed."

Now Laurie's fingers loosened again from the steering wheel as he pulled into the parking lot. The neon sign above the entrance glowed garishly into the darkness.

Melody reached out, her hand light on his shoulder. "Are you sure this is a good idea? Isn't this where you said you met . . ."

"Yes." He didn't let her finish the thought, remembering that first sight of Ryan with painful clarity. "I want a drink. Maybe a dance." He smiled wryly. "Humor me."

He slipped out of the car, walking around to get Melody's door for her. As they walked into the club, she reached for his hand, their fingers entwining.

The music surrounded them, enfolding them in the pulsing beat. Melody squeezed Laurie's hand as he silently led them to a table in a corner, within easy sight of the dance floor. "Two glasses and a bottle of red." He waved the waitress away quickly and settled in, slumping down in his chair.

Melody tried to talk, but he refused to answer, staring at the dance floor. When the wine arrived, he poured two glasses, handing one to her, and toying with the other, barely sipping at it.

She followed his line of sight to the twisting bodies on the dance floor. The music settled into a slower beat, and slowly the bodies resolved into couples, bodies linked and swaying. And everything made sense.

She had only met him once, but she knew who Laurie was watching. She reached out and covered Laurie's hand with her own. "Who is he with?" she whispered.

"Evan. He had just left Ryan when I met him." He slipped his hand free from Melody's and quickly downed his glass of wine, pouring another.

Out on the dance floor, Ryan caught sight of the table in the corner and smiled. Laurie couldn't help but smile in response. Ryan tugged at his companion's shoulder and they stopped dancing. It took a moment while Ryan drew Evan behind him through the crowd. Laurie took the time to compose his expression and his thoughts.

"Hi, Laurie." Ryan's voice was cheerful above the din of the music. "Evan, this is the wonderful friend I told you about."

"A pleasure." Evan's eyes reflected his confusion, a slight recognition of Laurie mirrored there. "Ryan told me how you encouraged him to give me a second chance. I'm grateful."

"Is it all working out?" Laurie was surprised his voice didn't sound more choked. It felt as if his throat were closed.

"Wonderfully." Ryan gave Evan an impulsive hug, his chocolate eyes showing desire. "It's better than before, and everything is out in the open." Evan smiled in response and their eyes caught. Laurie turned away slightly, unable to watch the silent exchange.

"I was overreacting, nervous," Evan admitted. "But I realized how much I missed Ryan, especially when I saw him at the theatre with you. I was so relieved when Ryan told me it was nothing serious."

Laurie quickly finished his second glass of wine. Melody frowned at his pale face, the faint red glow in his eyes. She poured him another glass of wine and quickly wrapped his fingers around the stem. His voice was soft, "I'm glad it's all going well."

"Thanks to you." Ryan slipped out of Evan's embrace. Giving Laurie a quick hug, he dropped a kiss on his forehead. "I really do appreciate everything you did for me."

Laurie reached up, his hand trailing briefly over Ryan's cheek before he jerked it away. "It was a pleasure." He swallowed hard. "If you need anything, you know I'll be there."

"I know." Ryan drew away, moving back close to Evan. As he slipped his arm around Ryan's waist, Evan leaned down and whispered something into his ear. Ryan's eyes lit up and he smiled back. "Let's dance," he whispered throatily.

"You okay?" Melody asked softly. Laurie's eyes were still fastened on the two men who had moved back onto the dance floor, bodies seeming glued together.

Laurie shook his head. "Let's dance." He dragged her out to the floor, fingers digging into her wrist. She slid into his embrace, wrapping her arms around him, hardly flinching when his arms pulled her roughly against him.

"I'm going to miss him." His words whispered softly against her cheek.

"I know," she said. "What happened?"

He shook his head. "I couldn't do it. He hated the idea of what I am. I had to let him go."

"He seems so . . ."

"I erased . . . changed how he felt about me." A tear rolled down his cheek, falling against Melody's. "I had to."

Melody caressed his back. "You still love him."

"Yes."

She pulled his head against her shoulder. Her hands stroked his back, comforting, drawing out his emotion. She could feel his shoulders silently heaving, the tracks of his tears soaking her blouse. While the music turned fast she continued to hold him and simply sway.

His Name Was Wade

Gary Bowen

His name was Wade, and he was tall and lanky and played
guitar like no man I ever saw. But when he opened up his
mouth and started to sing, that's when I lost it. I believe
in giving the Devil his due, and so I will say that Wade
was a handsome young man in a untutored, ranch-hand
kind of way, which of course the ladies liked. He was tall,
yet not over tall, he was lean, but not too muscular,
though his arms were ropy; and he had sandy blond hair
and an easy smile. It was the smile that really did it. The
rest of his features were pleasant enough, and many a
cowboy with a decent face and a sweet voice has tumbled
many a maid, but none of them could match Wade,
though at first glance he seemed to be yet another one of
them.

Like I said, it was the voice. I was standing there at the bar, doping myself with beer in order to withstand the coming amateur night, not expecting anything good at all. This bar wasn't even on my list, it was simply the place closest to the hotel. It was a coincidence that it happened to be having an amateur night and that I happened to be a talent scout/independent producer. Wade came out and took his place on a wooden stool with a microphone and acoustic guitar. One spotlight was on him, but nobody paid him any mind; there weren't more than a dozen people collected about the tables. None of them was there to hear some local boy with delusions of grandeur sing to them.

But they noticed. Not right away. They were slower than me. As for myself, all I can say is that when he moaned out the opening words, "Don't make me come to Dallas," a shiver went down my spine and a jumble went through my mind, which was half composed of, *I ain't going to Dallas for no man*, **and** *Damn, that boy's got a voice!* which then got melded into, *Gee, I wish somebody would sing that way for me.* I picked up my drink and ambled over to the stage, took a seat right at a front table, leaned back, and watched him sing.

He closed his eyes, didn't look at anybody, just leaned over that guitar like it was the only thing he loved and his fingers flew and strummed while the rest of him was so liquid it's a wonder he didn't slide right off the stool.

I know talent when I see it, and that boy had it raw, in spades, stacked to the ceiling, however you want to put it. I sat there with my heart in my mouth praying to God that he had more than one song in him. God knows how many promising boys and girls I've seen sing one, two, maybe even three pretty good songs, then punk out and flounder. A pretty voice sure is nice, but it don't pay the rent. Not all by itself it doesn't. There needs to be something extra, something that keeps them going, an obsession almost. Without it they might as well be singing in the church choir, because they aren't going to survive the record business.

The chords died away and the smattering of applause went up. I clapped harder than everybody, waiting with baited breath to see what he had next. He didn't disappoint me. Now that he'd hooked us all with the smoky power of his voice, he straightened up, looked me right dead in the eyes, and said, "Let's rock this joint." Maybe he looked at everyone in the house that way. In fact, knowing him now as well as I do, I'm sure he did. And that was the key to his magic; no matter how many people were in the room, no matter how absorbed he was in his music, he would give each person that piercing look that said, *This song is for you.* How they loved it. Women, hell, men, were sending him proposals for everything ranging from midnight trail rides to marriage and things that would get your arrested in fourteen states just for mentioning them. Sitting there in that bar my fingers itched for paper and pen; I wanted to sign him quick before he got away. I didn't examine my own motives too closely; the boy could sing, that was good enough for me. The rest was up to the starmaking machinery.

He had four songs, the maximum anyone was allotted in that place on amateur night. He played them all, and then he took his bows. His eyes raked over me like a poker raking up coals, and he then stepped down. The women mobbed him, but I was right up there with them. He gave me a cool look and accepted a lady on each arm. Pointedly turning his back on me he walked toward their table. I was not about to be rebuffed. I took a business card out of my wallet, and stepping around the redhead, I stopped in front of him and extended my card. "Call me if you want to make a record," I said. He looked at me, looked at the card, and didn't let go of either woman. "What kind of record?" he asked suspiciously.

"A hit record," I replied. "Ten thousand on signing. But I leave town tomorrow morning. You make up your mind." I tucked the card in his shirt pocket. He gave me a dirty look like he didn't like me getting that close to him, but he didn't say no. I touched the brim of my ten gallon hat, said, "Good night, ladies," and walked away.

"A record contract!" I heard one of them squeal. Then both of them were gabbing away at him.

I paused at the door and looked back in time to see him fighting his way clear of the women and retreating to the men's room. I stopped at the bar and ordered another beer, willing to linger long enough for him to catch me once he'd studied my card and decided I was for real.

I waited a long time. After half an hour I got worried and went to the men's room myself. He wasn't there. The hallways contained a door with a sign that said, EMERGENCY EXIT ONLY—ALARM WILL SOUND. I didn't try it, but I was willing to bet the alarm was turned off. *Damn. Now why would that boy run away from ten thousand dollars and a record contract?* I went back to the bar and asked the bartender, "What was that boy's name?"

"Wade," he answered. "Not sure what his last name is."

"He been here before?"

"Nope."

"He gonna be here again?"

"Maybe."

I was there for the next three amateur nights in a row, but Wade didn't show up. I cussed my luck and hated myself for not kissing up to him the way he seemed to have wanted me to, but damn, you can't kiss up to every two-bit talent that comes along because it doesn't pay off. But my bones were telling me that if I could land Wade it would pay off—big. If this boy turned out to be the next

Garth Brooks it would be worth all the ass-kissing. Real stars are highly individual, temperamental people. You have to take 'em that way because their strangeness is the seat of their genius. You take ordinary people, you get ordinary music. But damn, it sure was easier to deal with somebody sweet who could sing a pretty song. People would buy their albums, they just wouldn't buy as many as if the singer was something hot.

Then again, the hot ones had to be rescued from marrying their thirteen-year-old cousins and had to be bailed out for doing drugs and otherwise making life hell for their manager and ruining their label's wholesome image. Anybody who thinks Country-Western stars don't drink, do drugs, run around, cheat on their taxes, get in fights, wreck their cars, and hit their wives are dreaming. They just don't do it on stage like some other folks do. Not yet, though the way things have been going I expect to see it soon. Too many bad boys.

So I cussed Wade-without-the-last-name and told myself I was better off without a temperamental idiot that would drive me to distraction because no amount of money is worth that much aggravation. But I didn't believe it.

After I washed out three times at amateur night I started hunting him in earnest. Finally, a number of weeks later, I spotted the redhead he'd had on his arm oh-so-briefly, and tipping my hat to her said, "Honey, I remember you. You were with Wade."

Her eyes went all dreamy and she said, "Yeah." Her friends gave me funny looks, but she didn't seem to mind my intrusion.

"Do you know where I can find him? I'm with the record company."

She grinned happily and said, "He doesn't need a record, he's just *fine* in person." Her girlfriends tittered.

I pulled out a twenty. "Let me buy you all a round of drinks."

She took the money and said, "He's singing over at the Little Texas on Tuesday and Thursday."

The Little Texas was medium large for a dance hall and saloon. Wade was coming up in the world. He was still working the off nights, bracketing the Wednesday night karaoke, but that wouldn't last long. There was no cover fee; Wade was just some guy they'd hired so they could advertise LIVE MUSIC! He was their lip service to truth in advertising, but boy oh boy, they had hit a gold mine. The place was full, with only a few empty tables near the back. Definitely a good crowd for a Tuesday.

He sat up on his stool and a guy with a piano and a guy with a drum set backed him up. He wore a red satin cavalry shirt with shiny gold buttons and had a new black low-crowned cowboy hat on his head, but his black jeans were seriously worn and his boots were scuffed. I forced my way through the throng of admiring women and found myself standing along the wall with the men. Like I said before, women admirers were in the majority, but there were plenty of men who liked the way Wade sang. Or maybe it was the suspenseful way his torn jeans creaked as he moved. I discovered I was holding my breath in fear (or was it anticipation?) that the fabric would burst and he'd pop right out. Women singers had been playing that trick for years, so much so that when I met a woman in a gossamer lace top that seemed about to explode I paid it no mind because of course it never did. I don't know what they made women's things out of, but it only *looked* flimsy. In reality it was made of steel net, and however much a man might hope to get himself an eyeful, he never would. It took a long slow time before it percolated through my brain that Wade was playing the same game—and it was working just as well, on me and everybody else.

Wade held the microphone close to his lips and crooned, "Do you wanna dance?"

"Yes!" the women shouted back at him.

"Do you wanna dance with me, tonight, under the stars?" Maybe it was ad-libbed, or maybe it was carefully calculated. Whichever, it made the women go nuts, climbing up on the chairs and waving their hands, reaching out for those torn jeans that were just beyond their grip. Later we went on tour, and night after night he'd pull the same stunt, hunching close to the microphone, eyes heavy lidded, smoky voice asking, *"Do you want to dance with me?"* and every night it had the same electric effect.

Yes.

I was more than a little embarrassed to discover I had a hard on.

They played three sets. Mostly they covered popular hits, but added the raw sensuality most stars were too reticent to record. The piano player was competent; he banged out the honky tonk parts with vim. The drummer was good; he kept the rhythm—but neither of them was special. They followed Wade slavishly, simple accompaniments to his voice. After a time their inadequacy began to rub on me because there was nothing they were adding to the show except backup for the Voice. He didn't need them to do what he was doing, but he did need them because that's the way the business was. Guys just don't get up on stage all by themselves and sing. They have to have a band, a light show, a sound crew, they have to *entertain*. That was where I came in. But dammit, I had to catch him first.

So Thursday night I lay in wait for him, arriving early and camping in a dark corner until he and the other two

guys showed up and set up. Women were there, too, with
their discomfited boyfriends trailing in their wake while
the women fawned on Wade. He left the setting up to his
cohorts while he joined the women at their table and let
them ply him with drinks. I watched him carefully, and
discovered another trick of his: he never swallowed.
Instead he poured beer down one woman's bodice, making
her squeal. Her nipples stood up hard beneath the stretchy
green fabric and her boyfriend gave Wade a look that said
he was going to be dead in the alley in five minutes. Then
he licked her neck clean. He nuzzled her neck long and
hard and her eyes rolled up in her head. She slumped
against him, dreamy eyes gazing blankly. He smiled,
tapped her lips with his finger, then rose from the table
and went back to the stage. She lounged in her chair,
smiling like an idiot, blond hair sticking to the wetness
he'd left on her throat while her boyfriend glowered at
her.

I stepped onto the stage. "You need a bodyguard,
loverboy," I said. He looked around at me, glanced over
his shoulder at the jealous boyfriend, and said, "I'm doing
fine."

"What about that record contract?"

"No."

"No?" I gaped at him. "This lousy dirtwater band is
bringing in this many people and you say *no* to a record
contract? Are you crazy? Just think what you could do
with a real band!"

"I have a real band, and we do just fine. You can't do
what we do and have it come out right in a recording
studio. We're a live band." He ignored me real hard, and I
felt like I'd turned invisible. His back was turned to me,
and I was looking at broad red shoulders and a tight ass in
tight, worn jeans. His boots were silent as he cat-footed
across the stage trailing an electrical cord.

Then the drummer was at my elbow asking, "What contract?"

"I offered him ten thousand dollars last month."

"If he signs, do we all get signed?"

Not on their lives. Riffraff like them were a dime a dozen. I thought my answer over carefully. "If that's what he wants, that's what he gets." Now they would be on him like ticks on a hound, and they wouldn't let up until they had drawn blood.

The four songs he'd done at the amateur night were the only four original songs he had. Not enough for an album, but that didn't matter. I went back to my hotel, called Sully, and had him fax me three lyrics with melodies. When I got back to the bar, I folded them up and laid them on the floor by the drummer's foot. His eyes glowed like ball lightning and he almost missed a beat. I went back to the hotel and banged on my laptop until I had the contracts right. I was taking it upon myself to buy the rights to the songs from Sully, and it was going to cost me a pretty penny, which I was sure Wade would never reimburse me for. But I was willing to make an investment.

I didn't go back to the bar until Tuesday, Wade's next performance. I was dying to know how the drummer had made out; were they fighting over the new songs? Were they wearing him down, telling him not to blow his big chance? Or did he wad them up and flush them? Dammit, what did the man want?

Tuesday the place was packed. People were standing in line to get in, so I joined them and paid the cover. Yeah, management had wised up. They had even hung a sign on the front, WADE RAWLINS AND THE PARTY TIME BAND. Yeah, that summed up the act just about perfect. You wanna party, you wanna dance, you wanna rock this joint? Wade's your man. All those baby boomers fed up

with the nihilism of rock would jump ship to party with
Wade. I was about to burst an artery; I could taste the
success. So close. *Sign, Wade, sign.*

Wade came out on stage in a different pair of torn blue
jeans and a red satin shirt with white fringe on it. Same
beat up boots; this boy knew how to blend country hick
with city boy and they ate it up. I raced three other guys
for a vantage point near the right corner of the stage, and
by virtue of being bigger and older than any of them,
claimed the spot. I was chain-smoking cigarettes, a filthy
habit that would kill me if Wade didn't kill me with
musical blue balls first. Wade's eyes flicked across me and
I knew he knew I was there. He fiddled around on the
stage for awhile, then standing up at the microphone,
turned his head and looked right at me, those black eyes
nailing me to the spot, "This next song is in honor of the
most persistent man I ever did know." Then his eyes left
me and I could breathe again. He started singing *"Never
say no,"* the tag line from one of Sully's songs. Just him
and that glorious voice in a bar packed with silence. He
sang the refrain once through, then the drum rolled
underneath his voice, and suddenly the guitar wailed and
we were off on a completely different arrangement than
the one I had sent him. He'd taken a lovely ballad and
turned it into the wail of the damned, and I'd never seen
anything like it. My jaw dropped, my ears ached, and
every eye in the place was glued to him, and I don't think
anybody dared breathe. What had been a fairly clever song
about a young man desperately trying to talk a girl into
dancing with him became a whole lot more, and when he
got to the final line, *"You never said no, but my heart
said yes,"* the women started screaming. They never shut
up either.

After the show was over he walked across the stage and
said, "I want to talk to you." I nodded and he climbed

down. He never looked back, and I glanced at his cohorts. They were staring after him, worried looks on their faces. I'd be worried if I was in their shoes too; Wade might sign without them, or he might blow me off yet again. Either way, it didn't look too good for them to catch a ride on the magic carpet.

I followed him as he walked out of the bar. He ignored the people reaching out to touch him and offer him drinks and kisses. I followed along in his wake, gulping in cool night air when we reached the parking lot. "Take me to your hotel," he said.

I unlocked the rented Cadillac and he climbed in the front seat, then I let myself in. I didn't dare speak, I was pretty sure he was going to sign and I didn't want to do or say anything that would make him change his mind.

"You're a strange man," he said at last.

"Me? I don't think so. You're the strange one."

"You have no idea."

"I think I do."

"Do you? Do you know why I don't want to sign?"

My heart hammered in my chest. "No. I confess, I don't understand that."

"Because I'm a fraud. I'm only good in person, up on the stage. Did you notice the crowd as we left, how it got thinner at the back, how the people up front were practically slobbering on me while the guys in back didn't even notice me walk past?"

Now that he mentioned it, I sorta had. "That's obvious. The biggest fans always crush to the front. The crowd sorts itself out."

"I don't think I could please a crowd much bigger than that one. I certainly don't think you can record that kind of effect on an album either."

"Recordings never do justice to the artist," but I was pondering what he said.

"I don't think I could handle the energy of a larger crowd even if I could please one. It's a two-way street. I get energy from them, and I give it back. It's such a personal thing. I don't know if you understand that."

"I understand." I was sweating under the sport coat. I'd felt the power of his eyes, and now, with him caged in the interior of the car with me, I felt the power of his body. Magnetic. I wanted him to sign the damn contract and a whole lot more. Which was strange of me, because while I've got no objection to what other people do, I never thought I'd be tempted that way myself.

"Do you?"

"Yes, I do. It's why I want to sign you. You've got that intimate primal connection. You're afraid you're a freak. Well, maybe you are, in the sense that you're different from ordinary people. Stars always are. We can handle it. You'd be amazed at what you can do in a studio. It'll translate."

"Maybe that would be a real bad idea. What if whatever it is I've got can be packaged and sold like a drug? What then? You've already seen the Wade junkies."

"Everybody has groupies."

He was looking at me doubtfully. "You act like you've seen it a million times before, but you haven't. Trust me on this one. You have no idea what you're chasing."

I was pulling into the hotel parking lot. "Come upstairs. Sign. I appreciate you being honest about your doubts, but I know the score. Every new act is a risk, and most of them fail. One record, then poof, they disappear. But hell, even if that's your fate, wouldn't you rather give it your best shot than to spend the rest of your life wondering what you could have done if you'd gotten the chance?" He got out of the car without speaking. He followed me up to my room, his satin flashing under the fluorescent lights. It almost seemed to be reflecting, as if he was a puddle casting back the light he couldn't absorb. I unlocked the door, and he stepped past me into the room. I stepped in and shut the door, the lock snapping shut automatically. When I turned around again he was stripping off his clothes.

A good many things went through my mind, not the least of which was pleasure, followed by panic in close second. "You're queer?" I asked stupidly.

He glared at me and stretched his catlike body out on the bed. "Do I have a choice? Everybody wants me. Especially you. Well, now you've got me. What are you gonna do?"

Run like hell, the wiser part of my brain said. His eyes blazed at me. My cock was twitching, and I didn't run. "You misunderstand me," I lied. I had a lump in my throat, and another lump lower down.

He smiled that slow curving I-have-what-you-want smile, and I crossed to the bed and sat down. Then he was kissing me, and it was like making love to a jaguar: quick, lean, and fierce. He hurt me in several small ways, then in one large way, but it didn't matter because his mouth was on my neck and his weight was on my back and I was coming with an intensity the like of which I had never known before. I lay limp, incapable of moving, eyes staring dreamily. My neck stung faintly, and I knew he'd done to me whatever he'd done to the women.

I dragged a hand up to my neck and pressed it against the tiny wound. He dressed quickly, glancing at me. "You'll live," he said as if to reassure me. It hadn't occurred to me that I might not.

I dragged myself into a semi-sitting position. "What did you do to me?" My lips were numb as if I'd been shot full of Novocaine. He watched me warily as if he wasn't used to his prey getting up after he'd—he'd what? Fed? He had his jeans and shirt on and was pulling on his boots right quick. "Don't leave me."

"You'll be okay. You'll sleep it off. You'll have a headache. I didn't harm you." He was rushing to the door. Not that he seemed to hurry, maybe it was my own sense of time that was screwed up. "Sign, dammit," I said.

He stopped short. "Sign?" he asked in surprise.

Limply I pointed at the papers laying on the table. My head was reeling in a way that might have been pleasant if I was trying to get drunk. Slowly he returned to the table. He gave me a dubious look, then started reading the papers. I wished to God he would just sign the damn thing, but he didn't. He was going to continue torturing me with delays.

"You sure you want me to sign this?"

"Yes."

His hand hovered over the pencil. "Don't you want to know what I am?"

I was curious, but in no mood to let myself be distracted. "Sign, then we can talk."

He signed. I sighed with relief and flopped back down on the bed, feeling much too old and paunchy to be taking on a hellraiser like him. He straddled me, sitting on my pelvis, and opened his mouth. He stuck out his tongue and a stinger or fang like a very thin wire unfolded from under his tongue. He lowered it and touched it to my nipple and an electric shock bit my nerve. I jumped and twitched, then he worked that stinger all over my nipple. When his mouth finally closed on it, cloaking the nerves with warm soft relief, I discovered I had another hard on. This time when he slid down my body he let me feel his stinger as much as his kisses, and when he took my cock into his mouth I screamed. He didn't let go, and it hurt so good my hands tore the coverlet.

"Wade," I said afterwards. "You don't have to fuck your manager to get a contract."

He lay down beside me. "It's what everybody wants. I always had a pretty good voice and could play a guitar, but when this happened to me, well, hell. Sex." What he said was true, his fans were all made horny as sin by his voice and every one of them would gladly be in my place. Except me. I was a little sorry I'd let him seduce me like that, but I was also certain that I wouldn't have believed or understood how it was with him if he hadn't. I suspected I wouldn't have been able to resist, even if I had really wanted to.

"What happened to you?"

"Pretty much what I did to you. But it was a woman that did it to me. Why none of my partners wakes up with a stinger in their mouths I don't know. Maybe it's like getting pregnant: it could happen any time, but it really only happens once in a while."

I checked my mouth quick. "Don't you believe in safer sex?"

"It's kind of hard to stop having a mouth."

"Well, you shouldn't fool around so much."

He sighed heavily. "I can't eat anymore. When I sing, they come to me. I take a little bit from each one, and that's how I live. It goes to my head sometimes. I don't want to hurt anyone, and I don't want to lose control. Any bigger crowd—"

"We'll keep you fed. There won't be any reason to lose control."

He rolled over and pressed his mouth against my shoulder. The stinger jabbed and I flinched. It looked like I was the main entree until I figured out a way to keep my strange star satisfied. "I want you in the studio on Monday." Faced with the impossible, my brain took refuge in solving the merely difficult.

"Whatever you say," he mumbled against my chest. Then his tongue was dancing across my pecs, alternating kisses with stings. I was already worn out from his advances, but he seemed as lively as a puppy chasing butterflies. I was definitely too old for this. But like it or not, I'd chased him and now he'd caught me. I let him do what he wanted for the rest of the night. I wished I could say I didn't enjoy it, but that wouldn't be the truth.

Dedicated to Wade Hayes, my genuine cowboy man. It's a good thing they can't bottle that Voice, or I'd be drunk every night.

Katje
David May

As the serpent said, "Why not?"

—George Bernard Shaw

When Uncle Bas died and left his little house in Amsterdam (just south of the Jordaan and west of the Prinzengracht) to his nephew in America, the news was greeted among the cousins with knowing looks, the nodding of heads, and countless shrugs. Barry, after all, was "like his uncle," wasn't he? This was certain knowledge for Barry, like his uncle, had never married, but had for years brought the same young man with him whenever he visited his family in the Netherlands.

Since Barry had clearly been Uncle Bas's favorite, no one questioned the terms of the will, but discussed instead whether Barry would move all the way from San Francisco to the wicked city of the north, or ask one of his cousins to act as agent in the selling of the house in order to pay the heavy taxes on such an inheritance. The news of his decision to come and live in Amsterdam, after having received a huge sum in life insurance from the death of his "friend" (more than enough to pay the taxes and live comfortably for some time), was greeted with less than unbridled enthusiasm. Still they accepted it with the usual best wishes, however formal, they'd offer anyone, American cousin or not, who came to such good fortune through the misfortune of others.

Barry moved into the little house, only a few meters wide and perhaps twice as deep, with more luggage than seemed necessary to his more austere relations, explaining that some other things (his books, his CDs, and the odd bit of memorabilia) were being shipped. The furnishings and appointments of the house, he explained to his disappointed relations, he would keep as they were for the time being.

Barry insisted on speaking Dutch now, wanting to improve his grasp of the language he had learned in the nursery but had never taken further than the kitchen. He practiced speaking in the shops he frequented in the Jordaan, learned to ask for so many kilos of fruit or cheese, greeted the woman in the coffee shop on the corner, hoped each day to chat with the handsome man who lived across the street and undressed each night in front of his open window.

A small flower garden, narrow but long enough to get some afternoon sun, lay behind the house. A small tree grew there, old and solid, whose branches reached past the bedroom window on the second floor. In this garden, true to his mother's heritage, Barry spent much of his time raising flowers and preserving the work Uncle Bas had done there over the years.

Neighborhood cats came and went, passing through the garden without comment or even responding to his call of "*Poes, poes, poes.*" One cat though, a handsome brown tabby, would come to him, often without being called. More endearing still, he would jump from the tree through Barry's open bedroom window and sleep with him. Being lonely, having just lost the love of his life and knowing no one in the city but a favorite aunt and a handful of cousins that he'd never much taken to, Barry welcomed the cat's visits. He guessed the cat had been friends with his uncle, and greeted the visits as a bridge between them, a continuity between the generations.

Working in his little garden one day, he looked up to see the cat sitting on the fence and staring at him, slowly blinking his great orange eyes in greeting.

"Hey, *katje*! Glad you're here. Tell me," he whispered as one conspirator to another, "did I make a mistake coming here? I wanted a new start, but I forgot how hard it is to make friends in a strange city. And I'm not a kid anymore, *katje*. I'll be forty in a few years. Maybe I should go back to California? I still have a few friends left there. What do you think?"

Blinking his orange eyes, the cat walked casually towards Barry and rubbed against him. Then, with a few graceful leaps he was up the tree and meowing for Barry to open the bedroom window for him. Barry laughed as he got up to obey the cat's demand.

Maybe a few months was too soon to tell whether or not this was a good idea. He needed to give himself some time, he reasoned, time to make new friends and find his niche in the city he was now calling home. After all, it had only been a year since Josh had died. He and Josh had talked a lot about living in Amsterdam, and now he was living out their dream alone. For Josh's sake, at least, it seemed right to stay. Besides, he reasoned, climbing the narrow staircase, he'd already buried Josh's ashes in the garden and it would be such a bother to move them again.

Opening the bedroom window, Barry leaned out to appreciate the breeze gently rocking the leafy branches of the tree. With a small meow to warn his host, the cat jumped to the window sill where he sat looking expectantly at Barry. Stroking the cat and looking out towards the rooftops of Amsterdam, he felt a stirring deep in his gut, a longing for the companionship of the men who'd died and left him behind. That night, he decided, he'd meet a man and hold him close again, even if it was only for that one night.

He decided to live.

It was sometime before midnight when Barry was walking down Saint Jacob Straat and saw Ander leaning against his bicycle in the narrow street. Ander was as dark as Barry was fair, bearded, with a compact solid body, a youthful face and ancient eyes, eyes not quite natural even in the dimming summer twilight.

They nodded to each other, each saying hello.

"I'm Barry."

"You're American but you speak Dutch?"

"My mom's Dutch. She came to the States after the war with my Dad. My dad's Irish, which makes me American," he added proudly. "And you?"

"I'm Ander," he said after a pause, as if pulling the name out of the air.

"Can I buy you a beer?"

"*Alstublieft.*"

Once they were inside the Web, Barry leaned over the bar, automatically stroking the resident cat sitting on the stool by the cash register.

"*Twee biertjes, alstublieft.*"

Barry handed the beer to Ander.

"Your Dutch is very good."

"Not really. I don't speak it nearly as well as I'd like. I understand it pretty well, though."

They raised their beers in a toast.

"Groetjes!"

Barry continued to casually stroke the cat as they spoke, ignoring Ander's wary glances in her direction. It wasn't until later, when Barry reached over to kiss Ander and the cat hissed, striking at Ander, that Barry even noticed Ander's aversion to the creature.

Ander jumped back from the attack, smiled awkwardly and said, "Cats don't like me."

"Really? Then let's move on."

Out again on the narrow street, Barry did kiss Ander, felt his own blond beard rub Ander's black beard as their lips touched and their tongues tangled together.

"Where are you staying?"

"Near the Jordaan. I have a place there."

"Your own?"

"Inheritance," shrugged Barry. "Uncle Bas never married, so. . . ."

"How fortunate."

"That he left it to me? Yes. Rather like meeting you."

Ander's eyebrows arched in answer, as if to say, *You never know.*

They walked the moonlit streets to Barry's house, stopping occasionally to kiss in the shadows left by the moon wafting through the trees lining the canals.

Barry led Ander upstairs and stripped out of his clothes as soon as they were inside. He wanted to feel all of Ander, all that had been promised in Ander's kisses. Now naked, he saw how Ander's olive skin was covered with dark hair, his dick and balls pendulous as if bursting with seed even when soft, filled with the stuff of life. In all his years, Barry had never known such desire, a desire not so much for Ander, whose beauty was obvious but not irresistible, as for the ecstasy promised in all the kisses they'd shared since Saint Jacob Straat.

Their bodies lunged together, Ander's kisses spurring Barry on, clouding his mind with the need to possess Ander, to consume, and then be a part of him. He was trembling with excitement, fumbling with the condoms in the dark. He started to put a condom on his turgid cock when Ander's hand stopped him.

"No," said Ander. "It must be real or not at all."

"But you don't know me. I'm—"

"It must be real."

Startled, Barry obeyed even though he knew better. Maddened by desire, he could only comply with Ander's demands. He lifted Ander's legs over his shoulders, aimed his long, erect cock at Ander's butt hole, and entered him in a single magnificent stroke. The tight hole wrapped itself around his cock, sucking and pulling on it with an unnatural control.

Barry fucked Ander, fucked him with a fury and a passion. Their mouths met again and again to kiss as they fucked, the kisses spurring Barry on to fuck Ander harder and longer. Finally, unable to hold back anymore, Barry exploded, felt his balls burst as his seed poured out of him and filled Ander's ass. He collapsed on top of Ander, felt Ander's kiss as their lips met again. And then he saw Ander's satisfied smile, the smile of beast of prey content with his kill.

That night Barry dreamed of Ander.

Ander lay naked in the darkness, illuminated by the moon, his body stretched across an invisible surface. A huge snake wrapped itself about Ander. At first Barry thought that the serpent would kill Ander, strangle him in its death grip, absorb all his body heat. Barry wanted to call out to Ander, to warn him of the danger. But when Ander's eyes opened, his eyes were like the snake's. Then Ander turned into the snake himself and slithered away and out of Barry's dream.

Barry woke with a start, sweat pouring over his body and soaking his sheets. He looked about the room in a panic, not sure where he was or what time it was. A moment later, as his breathing quieted to normal, he was able to orient himself to his surroundings again, to remember where he was as he forgot the dream. Sunlight poured through the window, telling Barry it was already late afternoon. The cat sat on the branch outside his window crying to be let in.

Stumbling to the window, he saw that it was open a few inches already, even though he remembered closing it all the way to keep the cat from disturbing them. Forgetting his puzzlement a moment, he lost his balance, almost falling to the floor. Then, recovering himself, he pulled the window open only to fall back on the bed exhausted from the effort.

The cat jumped through the window in a single self-confident leap. Yowling his annoyance, the cat searched the room, then ran down the stairs to inspect the rest of the house, returning a moment later to Barry's bed. Nuzzling Barry's face, licking the damp skin, and purring loudly, the cat egged Barry out of bed and down the stairs, circling his feet until they were in the kitchen. Thinking the cat wanted to be fed, Barry offered him some cheese. The cat only cried again and again, staring at Barry with his huge orange eyes. Only when Barry sat down to eat himself did the cat sit quietly.

"Why am I so tired, *katje*?" asked Barry a few minutes later as he sat down to coffee and toast. "And where did Ander go?"

The cat hissed.

"Okay, *katje*. Sorry."

He got up to pour himself some more coffee.

"Cream, *katje*?"

A small meow.

"He said he didn't get along with cats. Nothing personal."

He sat down and watched his friend lap up the cream. All the while he ate, though, the cat kept an eye on Barry.

"Why am I so tired? Wasn't I supposed to do something today? Oh yeah, I'm supposed to meet *Tante* Dora for dinner. But I'm so tired, *katje*."

Another meow.

"I suppose you're right. I better shower first, though."

It wasn't until later, when he was walking toward Leidsekruis Straat to meet his aunt, that he realized that he'd been having a conversation with a cat. Even more puzzling was finding that the front door was still locked from the inside, leaving Barry to wonder how Ander had let himself out.

He greeted his aunt with three kisses, saying in Dutch, "Tante, sorry I'm late. Please forgive me."

"Of course," she answered in English.

"Nederland, Tante. Alstublieft."

"As you wish," she answered in Dutch. "Are you all right? You don't look well."

"Just tired, I think. Maybe I'm working too hard."

"Working at what? Have you a job?"

"No, Tante. I mean working on the garden, the house."

"Yes, of course," she answered unimpressed.

The waitress came and they ordered their meal.

"No, you don't look well, at all, dear," said Aunt Dora a moment later, reaching across the table and touching his face. "You feel clammy and a little warm."

"Maybe I caught a little cold last night. But it's nothing to worry about. I'm okay, Tante, really."

She took his hand across the table.

"I have to worry, dear. You're mother's not here to worry for me."

Barry smiled at his aunt a moment before changing the subject.

"Did Uncle Bas have a cat?"

"No, I don't think so. Why?"

"There's a big tomcat that likes to visit me sometimes. He acts like he belongs there so I let him come and go as he likes. I just thought maybe he was Uncle's cat."

"Probably just a neighborhood cat your uncle fed sometimes," said Aunt Dora. "He always had a soft spot for strays."

"Like me, Tante?"

"Well, you needed a new home didn't you?"

After dinner, Barry walked his aunt home before heading back to Saint Jacob Straat. It was early yet, the twilight still an hour or two away. He walked up and down the street a few times before heading back to the house. He'd come back later, he decided, and find Ander again. He felt the logy feeling that had been plaguing him since he'd woken up fade away. He brightened thinking of Ander, thinking of how much he wanted all that Ander had to give him.

Ander appeared from the shadows near the Milk Maids' Bridge. Stepping from behind a tree he came toward Barry, smiling, his eyes almost glowing with pleasure.

"Are you happy to see me?" asked Ander with his seductive smile.

"Of course!"

"Good!"

Ander's mouth reached up toward Barry's, his tongue darting forward as if seeking the warmth of Barry's mouth. For less than a second Barry remembered an image from his dream the night before. He started mid-kiss, then shook off the remnant of the lost memory as he lost himself in Ander's kiss.

Ander pulled Barry into a narrow side street and deep into its shadows. Wordlessly, he undid Barry's trousers. A moment later he was kneeling in front of Barry, sucking on the stiff cock sliding in and out of his wet, silky mouth. Too startled to resist, and excited by the circumstance, Barry held the back of Ander's head as he fucked Ander's face.

Barry shuddered each time Ander's tongue tickled the underside of his cock, gasped when Ander's throat opened and closed around his member, effortlessly enclosing its considerable length and thickness. Again, Barry tried to hold back, tried not to come so soon. His body shuddered as he clenched his butt and slammed his crotch against Ander's face. He felt himself shoot, lost in the sweetness of the orgasm, felt Ander swallow each shot of semen as it filled his mouth.

Then, just as he felt himself sink once more into oblivion, he heard a scuffle, the sound of a cat snarling in the darkness. Ander cried out in pain, and as suddenly as he had appeared earlier, slipped noiselessly into the shadows.

Barry slumped to the cobbled stones of the street and searched the moonlit darkness for Ander, whose kiss he already wanted again. Then he saw him, there on a doorstep, quietly washing his paws and glancing in his direction, a huge marmalade cat with luminescent green eyes.

"*Poes?*"

The cat stepped over to him at a relaxed trot. He looked up into Barry's face a moment before touching Barry's nose with his own and giving it a lick.

"*Dank, poes*. But what happened?"

The marmalade tom continued to nudge him until he got to his feet, then trotted along beside him until they crossed a bridge. With a small mew, the cat turned back to his own territory, leaving a large but dainty calico to lead Barry the rest of the way to his house.

"*Dank U, mevrouw poes*," said Barry, unlocking his door to discover his own katje sitting on the stairs in anticipation. "You two know each other or something?"

The cats saluted each other with raised tails, touched noses, and rubbed against each other. Then, as if on cue, the calico disappeared into the night.

"I'd like to know what's going on, *mijnheer kat*, but I'm too tired to understand anything that's happened to me tonight."

Exhausted, Barry climbed the narrow steps to his bedroom, followed by the cat.

The next morning he was shocked to see twice as much gray in his hair and beard than had been there a few days before.

Barry didn't see Ander again. Weeks passed into early autumn. He finally met the man across the street, whose name was Jan, and found himself slowly forming a friendship with him. Jan was taller than Barry, just as fair, handsome and leanly muscled. He was clean shaven but had the heavy kind of beard that showed stubble a few hours after shaving. His yellow-green eyes sparkled when he laughed, or when he talked about Barry's uncle.

"You know," ventured Barry rather cautiously one afternoon over coffee. "I can see you when you undress at night. Not that I mind."

"Yes? Your uncle always said he enjoyed watching me. Do you?"

"Very much."

"What should we do about it?"

"This?" Barry leaned across the kitchen table and kissed Jan, slipping his tongue into Jan's waiting mouth.

"You have safes?" asked Jan a few minutes later between kisses.

"Upstairs."

Running up the narrow stairs, they stumbled onto Barry's bed, undressing each other between kisses, pulling on each others' clothes. Rolling naked together on the bed, their muscular frames and thick cocks open to the other's caresses, each sought the secret spot that would drive the other over the edge, giving him the power. Jan won.

Nibbling and sucking on Barry's neck flipped the switch, sending waves of pleasure over Barry's body and forcing him to open himself up to Jan. Jan's hand found its way to Barry's fuck hole as Barry thrashed under Jan's hard, furry body. Spreading his legs apart, Barry wordlessly begged Jan to fuck him. Answering Barry's silent plea, Jan pulled a condom over his fat, uncut dick, then greased his cock with one hand while he prepared Barry's hole with the other. Lifting Barry's legs over his shoulders, he entered Barry.

Arranging his body so their faces touched, Jan moved his hips in and out, plowing the tight hole, filling it again and again with his prong. Barry threw his ass into the air, trying to hold onto Jan's cock with it, not wanting to ever be without it again, his head rolling back and forth in time to Jan's thrusts. Finally, grabbing Barry's face in a kiss, Jan slammed harder and harder inside Barry's hole, releasing the kiss only when he arched his back, and with a growl, filled the rubber with cum. Seconds later Barry's seed splashed all over them, sticking to their sweaty bodies.

When he finally got up to towel off, Barry could swear he heard Jan purring.

It was raining when Barry got in that afternoon, so he shut the bedroom window without thinking of the cat and hurriedly toweled the floor dry. He'd spent the afternoon helping Aunt Dora with a few repairs around her flat near Leidse Straat. He was running late now and needed to get ready for his dinner date with Jan. Aunt Dora had greeted the news of Barry's new romance cheerfully enough, saying she already suspected something of the kind. She even suggested that they all have dinner together next week some time. Thrilled at his Aunt's good will, Barry could hardly wait to tell Jan about it.

Just as he was getting into a clean shirt, there was a knock at the door. Thinking that it might be Jan coming by to collect him rather than meet him at the restaurant as planned, Barry threw the door open prepared to wrap his arms around his new love. Instead of Jan, there stood Ander.

"Miss me?"

"Ander, I ..."

"Can I come in? It's raining."

"Of course, but ..."

Ander quieted him with a kiss as the door closed. The kiss filled Barry with all the longings he'd felt before, all the unquenched desire burning deep inside him again. Mindlessly, he led Ander upstairs to his bed. Once in Barry's bedroom, they undressed quickly without talking.

Unable to think at all in Ander's presence, Barry followed his impulses. He rolled Ander over onto his stomach and entered him in a single smooth thrust, not bothering to lube his cock first. Giving in to the need for

Ander's flesh, for Ander's kisses, Barry fell into the abyss. Unable to control himself, a few minutes later he was shooting deep inside Ander's round, furry butt, screaming in pain as he felt his entire being being sucked through his dick. Ander only smiled.

Barry looked into Ander's strangely reptilian eyes for only a moment before he blacked out.

Barry didn't hear the phone ring or the knock on the door a few hours later. He slept feverishly through it all, waking now again to find Ander's smiling face. He'd summon all his strength to reach up and kiss Ander's cold lips, then lay back exhausted. More hours passed and Barry woke to find his hard cock in Ander's mouth. Unable to resist the force of Ander's ministrations, he grabbed the back of Ander's head and fucked the warm, wet mouth until he came. Passing out again, he glimpsed his own hand, now covered with liver spots, like that of a very old man.

Hours passed into days. The phone rang and went unanswered, likewise the loud knocking at the front door. Barry roused himself only now and again for Ander's kiss, or to cum again in Ander's mouth. Even as he felt his life being drained from him, he could do nothing to resist the only comfort now afforded him.

He woke one afternoon to find Aunt Dora shaking him awake.

"Barry, you look awful! How long have you been sick like this?"

Barry tried to form the words to explain but couldn't.

"Drink this."

Barry sipped the warm broth being offered, smiled his thanks and drifted back to sleep. Whenever he woke up now he found his Aunt where Ander had once been. Each time she offered nourishment and each time he managed more of it, staying awake longer each time.

"I must have gotten the flu or something," he said when he was at last able to speak. "I just remember laying down and . . ." He faded off, not wanting to finish the thought, not wanting to remember what had actually happened.

"That's enough, sweetheart. I met your Jan today. He came to the door and I told him you were very sick." She looked down on Barry and smiled. "Your parents are coming, too, dear. They'll be so glad to see you looking better."

Barry turned away, pretending to fall asleep so she would leave the room, knowing that she was lying about his looking better. He could see his aged hands, feel his sagging skin and tired limbs. He'd seen his reflection in the mirror and knew how much he'd aged since he first kissed Ander. He was dying and knew it.

He heard his aunt get up and open the window, letting the late afternoon sunshine warm the room, and left. Barry inhaled deeply, enjoying the sweetness in the autumn air filling the room, and fell back asleep.

Later on it cooled and he wished Aunt Dora would come and close the window. He was about to call her when he heard an odd sound, a slithering and an almost silent hiss, then the sibilant call of his name. He turned in his bed to see Ander sitting in the window, naked, staring at him with his yellow reptilian eyes.

"One last kiss, my love, and it will be over."

Barry could only stare, certain he was hallucinating.

"Your kind is always so sweet, but you, Barry, are the sweetest," Ander went on. "The sweetest soul I've ever tasted. That's why I've taken so long. You're too delicious to rush. But now, sweet Barry, it's time."

With a sudden chill, Barry remembered his dream now, remembered and understood it. To his horror, he saw Ander become a snake, some eight feet long, almost a foot wide where it was thickest. He wanted to scream for help but couldn't. Instead, he curled into the far corner of the bed, waiting.

Then he saw the cat in the open window, tried to tell him to stay away with a wave of his hands, to at least save his uncle's friend. Just as the snake's almost smiling face appeared over the edge of the bed, Ander's yellow eyes now unmistakable, the cat streaked across the room like silent lightning. Attacking the serpent almost too quickly to be seen, the cat sunk its fangs below the snake's head. The cat shook the snake in his mouth, knocking over furniture, banging the snake's head against the wall again and again.

Suddenly the cat and the snake were both men, Ander and Jan. Jan tore at Ander's throat with his bare hands, breaking the neck, then tearing it off the body. Barry watched wide-eyed as Ander's severed body returned to its snake form, then shriveled to a mere pelt. Jan stood over his opponent, wiping his mouth with his pawlike hand before turning around to Barry.

Barry felt his strength returning, looked at his hands and saw the liver spots fade. Touching his body, he found the same hard musculature of years before. Strong enough now to sit up, he could see his reflection in the mirror across the room. The rapidly accumulated gray now faded to reveal the ash-blond hair and beard of his youth. Too startled to understand any of what had happened, he could only look about in confusion.

"Barry," said Jan leaping across the bed to hold him close. "Barry, you're safe now. He's dead."

"What was it? What are you? Have I died?"

"Quiet, sweetheart. Ssh. Rest. You need to sleep to recover. Daylight will be the final cure."

Whether from exhaustion or shock, Barry would never know, but he fell asleep in Jan's arms and stayed there the whole night through.

Jan woke him just before dawn.

"Come see," said Jan.

Turning back into a cat, he took Ander's snake head in his mouth and with a few leaps was on the roof across the way. Going to the window, Barry watched in awe as the morning sun crept across the rooftops. The cat Jan pushed the snake head into the sunlight, stepped back expectantly and watched as it burst into flames. A moment later Jan was back to fetch the pelt and do the same with it. Another burst of fire and it was over. Jan returned the second time smiling, pleased with his conquest.

"What was he?"

"I don't know what they call themselves, but they're as bad as bloodsuckers and live until they're killed by something stronger. Sometimes they even kill each other. I only know that they came from the desert like my folk. And like us they've followed humankind from place to place."

"And you, Jan? What are you?"

"I'm a cat," he said simply.

"Yes, but—"

"Ssh. Your aunt's coming."

Barry returned to bed as Jan quickly righted the furniture that had been knocked over in the struggle hours earlier. When Aunt Dora came in, Jan was a cat stretched across the bed and Barry was sitting up, bright eyed and alert, suddenly cured.

"Tante, I feel so much better today. And hungry. May I have a pancake for breakfast? You know how I like them, with apples and cinnamon?"

A few hours later, Jan came back by way of the front door, freshly dressed and shaved. Overcome with Barry's sudden recovery, and emotionally exhausted from thinking she was about to lose her favorite nephew so soon after she'd lost her brother, Aunt Dora gladly turned Barry's care over to Jan and went home.

"I still don't understand, Jan," said Barry looking into the mirror yet again, mesmerized by his sudden youthfulness. "What happened to me? I look even younger than I did before I met Ander."

"Some things don't need to be understood, my love, just appreciated."

"But why me? Why did Ander want me? He said something about my 'kind.' What did that mean? And you, why did you decide to watch over me like this?"

Jan looked at him a moment before answering, clearly puzzled.

"You really don't know, Barry? Your uncle understood, and he was only *fee* on one side. You're fee from mother *and* father."

"*Fee?*" asked Barry, in English this time. "You don't mean fairy?"

Jan nodded.

"You never knew?" asked Jan.

"This is just like the stories Granny Butler used to tell me. Maybe it explains why Josh and I . . ." He let his voice trail off, remembering how unlikely so much of his life had been.

"Then it is good you are here, *feeje*. There is much for you to learn. And as for why I'm here, I promised your uncle to look after you. And. . . ."

"And?"

"And I fell in love with you."

Jan kissed Barry on the neck as he said these last few words, touching that sweet and secret place that made Barry shiver. Barry automatically spread his legs apart as Jan's hand found his fuck hole, sending more shivers up and down his spine as Jan caressed it. A few minutes later they were naked on the bed, Jan's sturdy cock poised to enter Barry's tight hole.

Grabbing Jan's face as he was entered, Barry kissed his lover hard on the lips.

"Fuck me hard, *katje*! Fuck me hard!"

Jan smiled, purred, and obeyed.

A note about Dutch: Most of the Nederland (as Dutch is properly called) in this story is pretty self-explanatory, especially if you know even a little bit of German (though you should never confuse the two under any circumstances.) The Dutch have a charming habit of creating diminutives and endearments with the addition of je *on the end of a word. Kat, or cat, then becomes* katje, *or kitty. This is done with many everyday words, my favorite being when they turn* twee *(two) into* tweeje *when referring to a married couple or a pair of lovers.*

The Lunar Eclipse

Thomas S. Roche

The door to the Gallery is open to the street. Dark breezes blow through, rich with lilac blossoms, pregnant with the fruits of a Midnight Spring. The wind wanders aimlessly through the Gallery, caressing velvet draperies and black lace curtains, stirring ancient rose petals and dessicated leaves amid roaming ghoul girls and skeleton boys, will o' the wisps and Elviras, sprinkled liberally with art critics and the nouveau riche. The incense burner near the back gives off the odor of a Catholic funeral. Shimmering moonlight slants down from the paneled windows high above the Gallery floor. Gorecki plays from hidden speakers. Somewhere in the night a star has gone supernova and vanished, its death wail a pulsar beacon bathing the Gallery in radio waves. A poisonous spider spins its web behind the Gallery door.

A man in a black wool blazer and a turtleneck sniffs
disapprovingly at a painting of a naked white-skinned
beauty with eyes and hair the color of coal. The woman
on his arm tosses her hair, removes her sunglasses, and
peers forward, studying the oil painting with a collector's
grace, a critic's distance, an echoing hint of enthusiasm.

Her eyes narrow to slits; she thinks *such sadness* as if to
say it, then refrains. The wind picks up slightly. Rose
petals scatter about her feet.

"I like it," she says absently, as if to herself.

"Oh Marguerite," says the man, rolling his eyes. "Puh-
leeze!"

Marguerite shrugs and the two of them move on.

The CD player has shifted to Haydn, playing *The Seven
Last Words of Jesus Christ*. Occasionally the cry of a bat
splits· the night, mingling with cello and viola. High
above, there are leathery wings and tiny claws upon the
windowsil. Overhead the heavens spin in tortured
anticipation, rapturous preapocalyptic foreplay, for
tonight at 3:04:57 the city will experience its last lunar
eclipse of the century. Shadows flicker through the
Gallery.

Underneath, before a painting of a haunting ghoul girl, a
man in a trenchcoat and Roman collar crosses himself.
There is the distant sound of weeping.

The Gallery of Despair is open for business.

She wanders the darkness, drinking her fill of the lush
beauty of nightmares. She casts the paintings aside like
dead roses, her feet stirring their remains on the black-
painted floor.

The woman is shrouded in shadows and a black Chanel
overcoat, her black hair topped by an antique sort of
pillbox, her eyes and her face down to her lips covered by
the barest whisper of a fishnet veil sprinkled with black

baby's breath. Black lace mourning gloves cover her white hands.

The girl stands motionless before the painting, her eyes distant and moist.

Her hands are clasped before her. Her black dress swirls in the wind. She clutches an Addams Family lunchbox. She has black hair and pale skin. She is perhaps twenty-three. She is not quite weeping.

The woman stands just behind her and to the left, regarding the painting as well. The girl seems to sway before the work of art, as if hypnotized.

"Such sadness," murmurs the girl, as if to herself. She looks back over her shoulder briefly and sees the woman. Blushing red, she steps aside. "I'm sorry," she says nervously. "Am I blocking your view?"

"Not at all," says the woman, watching the girl. "My name is Cassandre."

"Cassandre," says the girl. "Do you like the painting?"

"Perhaps," replies Cassandre. "Perhaps not. It depends on how you look at it, as most things do."

"I suppose that's true," says the girl, as if it was an important truth. "My name is Andrea."

The woman nods, her full lips pursed underneath the black veil. "And you, Andrea. Do you like the painting?"

Andrea thinks a moment, and then she speaks as if in a trance. "The sadness is crushing. . . . It causes my soul to ache. It makes me feel my soul will be extinguished, the very life snuffed out of me. It is as if all life's subtle agonies and misfortunes are summed up inside it. . . ."

Cassandre watches, mesmerized. Her black lace fingers are crossed as if in prayer. Her eyes study Andrea, fascinated and enthralled. Her lips part slightly as if in the subtle prelude to a kiss. "Is that a yes?"

Her trance broken, Andrea blushes a still-deeper red. "I like the painting very much."

"You know . . . what happened? After the painting's completion?"

"Oh yes," says Andrea softly. "Such sadness."

"She was my sister."

Andrea's eyes are wide, the whites luminescent in the darkness. "The woman who—"

"The artist. Her name was Miriam."

"Of course, Miriam Sacramente. Your sister! How tragic for your family. . . ."

"I'm the only one left," says Cassandre sadly. "For the moment." She raises her hand to her temple, then quickly bites one finger as if wrestling with tears. "Our family has always been haunted by tragedy. But Miriam and I shared a bond. The mourning I feel is immeasurable." She sighs. "My sister was a . . . disturbed woman."

"And the model—?"

Cassandre shrugs. "I didn't know her."

"I think her name was Loren," says Andrea. "A friend of mine was in her acting class. Such sadness. . . ."

"Yes. Sadness. I miss Miriam most acutely. Some days I think I will shatter for want of her guiding hand. She was my elder sister, you see, and very much my mentor . . . though my sister and I differed on certain fundamental matters of artistic philosophy."

"You are an artist, as well?"

Cassandra smiles vaguely. "If you like."

"I'm studying at the University. But I fear I won't ever be this good. Talent like this is so rare. . . ."

"Skills can be learned. Miriam taught me so many things."

"But you differed with your sister? On matters of art?"

Cassandre regards the painting. "More on matters of . . . morality. Basic and fundamental morality."

Andrea's chin inclines, her eyes narrowing. She studies the woman, her body stiffening slowly as she processes the statement. Andrea nods gradually, turning to look at the painting, finding her gaze straying periodically to the back of Cassandre's head, the slope of her neck, the fall of the black hair on her collar. The woman is very expensively dressed, though with impeccable restraint. The black fishnet veil makes it plain that she is in mourning, not merely indulging in a fashion statement.

Andrea feels her breath coming quickly and imagines the glass of red wine that she and Cassandre might share in the Gallery Café across the street.

But alas it seems impossible if Andrea has correctly inferred what Cassandre's moral differences with her sister may have been—

"You differed from your sister," says Andrea sadly. "On moral grounds. . . . That must have been very difficult." Gently, fearfully, she asks, "Was this a . . . religious difference?"

Cassandre turns her head, eyes Andrea at a subtle yet distinctive, unmistakable angle. Faintly, she smiles, mischief twisting the edges of her full lips. "Perhaps it was, after all, a religious issue. Or, more properly, spiritual. We differed almost solely on issues of morality."

Cassandre's eyes hover darkly behind the veil. Her smile disappears and she tells Andrea, very softly, "On matters of taste, my sister and I were virtually identical."

Andrea finds her hand straying absently to her throat.

The seduction is achieved with a minimal number of words exchanged, a soundless apocalypse. Andrea orders red wine, Cassandre absinthe. The bored punk girl at the counter is listening to a very loud Rachmaninov, perhaps the ideal accompaniment to an irresistible invitation to a shared midnight of mourning. Andrea sips her wine as she and Cassandre quietly discuss art and experience—in vague terms considering the subtleties of various shades of

black and the beauties of the midnight wind, sharing
whispered speculations of the promises of lush mortality
within the corridors of the Gallery of Despair. Andrea's
second glass of wine remains untouched on the bistro
table as she feels Cassandre's fingertips travel onto her
wrist with an admirable subtlety. Andrea inhales, smelling
Cassandre's warm fragrance, a subtle mélange of exotic,
nameless wood scents and the perfumes of necrotic
flowers from genera long thought extinct. It is a
bewitching olfactory symphony that causes Andrea's nose
to tingle, awakened. With the finesse of an artist,
Cassandre touches Andrea's flesh, applying only the
lightest of touches, causing Andrea to goosebump all over.
The sensations of Cassandre's fingertips on her forearm
make Andrea's belly flutter, her throat tighten, her pulse
start to race. Andrea loses herself in the texture of the
seduction, recalling yesterday's sumptuous nightmares.
She becomes acutely aware of the proximity of Cassandre's body to hers, the pressure of Cassandre's bare
knees against her own. She feels the tension growing
between them over a progressively smaller space. She feels
the tangible desire welling in her body and conjures a
silent prayer that that desire is mirrored in Cassandre's.
And yet her whole body seems drugged, as if she is in a
delicious but frightening dream. The fear is almost too
much to bear, and Andrea continues staring down,
unwilling to break the spell Cassandre has cast by her long
silence. When Andrea does finally look up, Cassandre's
face is mere inches from her own, with blackberry lips
parted and tongue-tip extended almost imperceptibly—
and Rachmaninov surges in that final tempestuous
explosion as hopeless souls arrive on the bleak shores of
the Isle of the Dead, and Charon deposits them, laughing
cruelly; the souls, abandoned in a desperate orchestral
summoning, serve a delicate counterpoint to Cassandre's

lips locking magically onto Andrea's and parting just the appropriate amount. Cassandre leaves a bill on the table, giving the punk girl a large tip.

High above the city in Cassandre's rented loft, Andrea finds herself deliciously undressed. The huge loft is unfurnished except for a black-framed futon with a red velvet bedcover, a single white candle, and a tiny cassette player that issues forth a tinny rendition of one of Beethoven's string quartets. Cassandre has disrobed, except for the black lace gloves. First Cassandre's long lace-clad fingertips unfasten the front of Andrea's dress. Moonlight shimmers across the futon and the flesh of the naked Cassandre. Skilled fingers peel back Andrea's black lace dress and the black slip underneath, ease both over her shoulders, expose the white expanse of her throat, the slope of her breasts, her firm dark nipples with their steel rings. Cassandre's two suitcases are opened on the floor by the futon, containing scatterings of black lace and red velvet, with her black overcoat hanging by the door next to Andrea's leather jacket. The dress comes down easily, amid a gentle squirming of Andrea's body. The slip follows more slowly, accompanied by a faint prickling of Andrea's skin as it excites. The uncharacteristically haphazard manner with which Cassandre discards the dress and slip onto the floor heralds the approach of her ardor. Breezes stir the winds of the room, excite the flesh of Andrea's breasts, swirl Cassandre's perfume around Andrea's face. Surging forward, Cassandre takes Andrea's face in her hands and kisses her: insistently, demandingly, tenderly. Their tongues entwine and Cassandre feels the cold steel of Andrea's piercing.

Deliciously, she draws back at the summit of the kiss, creating a tension that grows as they regard each other.

Perhaps an inch now separates them, lips and eyes aching to touch.

Cassandre's fingers find Andrea's breasts, touching the nipples gently.

Andrea, dressed now only in her panties, reclines into the sumptuous red velvet bedcover as Cassandre rises to her knees and flows over her, not quite touching Andrea, not quite sliding on top of her. Instead, Andrea finds herself stretched amid red velvet as Cassandre's fingers entwine with hers, as their arms touch, as the fingers of Cassandre's other hand draw a path from Andrea's breast to her throat and then to her chin.

Cassandre lays on the bed beside Andrea, the length of her naked body very close to Andrea's but not quite touching. Andrea feels the touch of the fingertips on her chin, the inspecting caress of the path traced down, up, down, up, then down again, then finally up as Cassandre's fingertips take Andrea's chin and push her face, demandingly, to one side.

Andrea whimpers softly as she feels her throat exposed, feels the surge of blood and fear along the path Cassandre's fingertips have traced.

Then gradually, yet suddenly, comes the aching moment, the frozen seconds as Cassandre's mouth gradually descends, her blackberry lips parting sumptuously as their edges twist, her eyes sparkling. Cassandre savors the moment of surrender, the tension between their bodies explosive in the moonlight. The moment lasts for perhaps ten seconds in torturous and erotic desperation, but even so Andrea finds herself unable to scream.

The touch of Cassandre's mouth upon her throat is perhaps the most intensely spiritual sensation Andrea has ever known. The pain of the penetration feels inexplicably like ecstatic pleasure, and the warmth in her throat is unmistakably sexual while retaining a certain religiosity. Beside Cassandre and unrestrained, Andrea squirms, her body writhing freely on the bed, until Cassandre begins to stroke her smooth stomach gently; momentarily, the motion of Andrea's squirming body subsides.

Cassandre's left hand entwines Andrea's black hair and takes a firm grip on it, holding her tightly in position. A single bead of red makes its way gradually down Andrea's throat and onto her breast, pausing at the swell of her nipple, to be followed by the path of a second bead of red. Both rivulets then fall despairingly onto the bedcover.

Eagerly: Violin, second violin, cello. Viola.

Subtly, with the distinct but flattering taste of an afterthought, Cassandre's hand moves lower on Andrea.

Afterward, Andrea finds herself staring into Cassandre's expressionless face, seeing no trace of her blood on the vampire's lips. She recalls being dimly aware of the gentle stroke of a warm sponge on her breast, then on her throat. The sharp smell of antiseptic and the feel of the adhesive bandage brought back memories of childhood sickbeds. Cassandre's eyes flicker darkly in the starlight, for at this moment the moon has experienced its only remaining total eclipse in this century. Her fingertips trace the outline of Andrea's slightly parted lips; her tongue aches with the memory of the girl's taste and the texture of her surrender.

"You understand now," whispers Cassandre, "how I differed substantially from my sister on matters of morality—but certainly not on matters of aesthetics."

Andrea nods, faintly, her body very weak. She tries to speak, but it only comes out as a deliciously tortured moan. Cassandre lays a single finger gently on Andrea's lips and whispers, "Rest."

Morning finds the sunlight streaming through the skylight, caressing Andrea's body. The warmth dispels the weakness inside her, but slowly. It is not quite sleep that she experiences until late in the morning, but a delicious kind of trance, the sensation of her soul having been somehow purified of the indulgence of conscious thought.

Cassandre has left, offering only a note on parchment, written in fountain pen, cryptic only in its directness:

The loft belongs to a friend who is not expected back until early next month. Please stay as long as you like; there is food in the refrigerator, though you will find that my tastes run distinctly toward the sublime. I mustn't return—not for a time, at least. My thanks and affection always. C.

Andrea lifts the note to her face, inhales deeply of Cassandre's scent—indescribable, subtle, seductive. She lays on the bed, the parchment across her breasts, feeling strangely unbetrayed, yet oddly unfulfilled. There was, after all, no agreement, no suggestion of lovemaking to come, no promised nights of ecstacy and sanguine spiritual enlightenment underneath the lunar eclipse. Never an implication that any part of either of them would belong to the other, except for the blood which passed between them and the passion that blood had wrought. There was only the frozen moment when Andrea understood her devourment and knew, with a certainty that struck to the core of her being, that she was not going to be harmed. It was a certainty that Loren, Miriam Sacramente's beloved and unfortunate model, may have had at one time, but that certainty was unfortunately in error, as so many certainties are. This is perhaps the moral lesson that Andrea would have offered, given the chance to compose her own epitaph—but, thankfully, she was not yet offered that chance, nor that necessity, for Cassandre differed significantly from her sister—in matters of morality if not of art. And gothicka by moonlight offers its own kind of epitaph: a taste for the undead and, perhaps, a lingering appreciation of Rachmaninov. And what the hell, maybe a haiku, since it's morning:

> *She was kissed*
> *beneath the catharsis*
> *of the lunar eclipse.*

The Blood Hustle

Raven Kaldera

So I don't usually go under for johns, all right? I mean, I don't have reactions that are based in reality. If I get a hard on for them, it's because I'm thinking about something else. If I make noise, it's because I figure they want it. I do what they like, and I collect my pay, which isn't in money.

In a way, the only thing I do that's real is when I collect; I get my hands on their throats and get my fangs into their carotids so fast that they can't change their minds and stiff me. It's that bare minute of sincere pleasure as their lives flow into me that really turns me on, that gives me a hard on that isn't faked. I can never seem to control that desire, no matter how hard I try. Sometimes, when I pull away, I see a flicker of uncertainty in the trick's eyes, as if the reality of what I am—and what I'm not—has just flashed momentarily across their minds. All it takes is a touch from me, though; a softly spoken word, a caress, and they're back to their comforting illusion, the uncomfortable possibilities forgotten. Which is what I want, since illusions are my stock in trade.

More often I pull away to see their eyes glazed and gasping, especially the ones who've never been under the bite before. They might have heard about how good it feels, how you can get addicted to it, but they didn't really understand it. I never take anything that comes out of their mouths for the next hour seriously; they'd promise me their first-born children until they come down. The ones with a taste for it aren't as gullible, of course. They may want it bad, but they kick me out afterward to enjoy their nod in privacy. They know better. So it's what I do; I'm a very special kind of whore, but don't you think it's all that different in the end.

So I showed up at the hotel room to meet this guy— Tenny brokered the arrangement, told me he was OK— and waited. I was early; another appointment had fallen through and all the buses actually came on time. I ran through the Black Sun mantras in my head, the ones I learned from my sister in the discipline training of her religion. Yeah, that's right, DarkMother's Children, the Zavaret's little cult. *Thou shalt not kill except in self-defense, thou shalt not feed without consent*, and all of that. Or the "vampmonks," as the others call Black Suns. Of course, they have to hunt down their prey; mine sign up for the privilege. And they don't have our learned control; they're more prone to go crazy, kill people without meaning to. I don't always agree with my sister's rigid ethics, but I'm just enough of a control freak not to want to be ruled by the Urge.

It was getting l[...]
up to look out th[...]
the street when h[...]
and turned arou[...]
shoved in the po[...]
to the side, hip[...]
James Dean fa[...]
guys fall for th[...]
ripped cutoffs[...]
Vlad, the jack[...]
around my fo[...]
push-up bras[...]
Women are harder to p[...],
what they like, or hope they can take me [...]
I happen to be in.

He was short, slight, ordinary-looking. White-collar, at a guess, maybe educated, dressed down in newish jeans. He caught his breath when he saw me—good sign—and then ducked his head and hurried to the armchair across from me. I stayed standing. Let him get a good look. "So I'm here, man," I said softly, unthreateningly.

He cleared his throat and crossed his legs, just after I caught a glimpse of what he was hiding between them. "You know how you're getting paid?" he asked, his voice cracking.

I nodded. "Do you understand what that means?" I threw back. Best to get this part over with quickly.

His nostrils flared. "You tell me."

I looked away, phrasing my words carefully. "You don't get my blood," I said, toying with the Black Sun pendant around my neck. Tenny would have explained what it meant. "Believe me, you don't want it. I don't do piss, shit, or animals, and I don't do anyone else unless I negotiate with them separately." My gaze slid toward him; he nodded briefly. "And you're safe with me; I won't

Part of what allowed me to do
...ghness with which I had put about
...arkMother's Child, and my absolute
... tenets. It wasn't nearly as absolute as
...ggest, but no one needed to know that.

..references," he said, and then there was
...e looked me up and down more openly. "You
...d it bad," he said, and I resisted the urge to roll
...s. I was never hard up, but he wasn't the first trick
...it suited to believe that I was starving and desperate.
...iow long has it been for you?" he asked

I bared my teeth in something that might have been a smile but wasn't. "None of your fucking business," I said pleasantly.

He looked startled, and then laughed. Good, a sense of humor. A rare find in johns. "You're hot," he said, a thread of longing in his voice. "I haven't been with a guy since high school."

"Why?" I asked, shifting my pose to show the outline of my cock against the denim cutoffs.

"None of your fucking business," he retorted, and then stood up and came toward me. He was hard, all right. "What are you hiding back there? Turn around, I want to see you," he ordered. I grinned and did it, letting him get a view of my ass and my waist-length hair. He came up behind me and ran his hands through it, buried his face in it. "Gorgeous," he mumbled. "You smell so good."

"Not at all like the grave," I quipped, looking up at the ceiling. He seemed a little unsure of what to do next, so I put my back to the wall and pulled his hips to mine. I let him lean into me, let the front of his jeans press against mine as he kissed me. He smelled of toothpaste; I was touched.

The guy clung to me like he hadn't had human contact in years. Hell, maybe he hadn't. His tongue explored my mouth, but fortunately my fangs weren't unsheathed. My hands drifted from his ass to his hard on, and he groaned, so I turned us around and pushed him up against the wall; then I went down on my knees and opened his fly.

There are several ways to get through a blow job without massacring your throat; for example, after a while it gets easy to tell if whether a guy is the type who shoots off right away or takes his time. This guy was definitely in the former group, and he had a little dick too, small enough that I could nearly cover it in my hand. I know queers are supposed to like big dicks, but the only place I like a huge salami is on myself, which fortunately I was blessed with. Feeling charitable and pleased with this trick, I gave him the standard all-out deepthroating, keeping one hand on his ass while I unzipped my cutoffs and got out my own cock with the other. I don't think it took him more than three minutes to give a hoarse cry and shoot off in my mouth. Good, This would be an easy one.

He was still panting and gasping when I stood up and removed my cutoffs, and this time I leaned into him, letting my cock brush his. I was conveniently hard, mostly from a little judicious fantasizing while I had been slurping his dick and he got hold of it and stroked it gently. I actually like a little harder stimulation than that, as mine wasn't as sensitive as his obviously was, but I let myself be teased by the light touch. "What else do you want?" I whispered. "You're paying for the fuck."

"I want more of what I see now," he whispered back. "Lay down."

OK, I got it. You'd be surprised how many tricks want to suck cock, as well as or even instead of being sucked off themselves. Especially the ones who are weird about being queer, so that going down on some guy is the ultimate taboo, one they have to pay an anonymous stranger to experiment with. Not to mention that a guy who's getting paid isn't going to complain about their technique. My trick took a deep breath. like he was nerving himself up, and then sank his mouth onto me. Unlike the nearly effortless blow job I'd given him, he had a little more trouble with my size and his obvious lack of experience. My cock, however, is well-trained enough to come almost when I tell it to, and on all kinds of stimulation. Since I died and came back, it isn't quite the center of my sexuality in the way that it used to be, and I have more control over it. Or I like to think so, anyway, most of the time.

Somewhere along the line, he got a finger between my ass cheeks and tickled the fur on my butt, and that put me over the edge with a suddenness that startled me. I don't ejaculate, and he looked a bit surprised as he came up off me. I lay there bemused and wondering what had just happened. "Turn over," he said, an excited gleam in his eye. He was hard again. Yeah, this was one of the Alexander Portnoy types, shoots off in three minutes and gets hard again in another three, makes up for lack of staying power with continual repeat ability. I got on my knees, ass in the air, which is as much a part of the fetish for these guys as the leather jacket and the attitude. The ones who wanted delicate fresh young things with trembling lips weren't going to want to fuck a vampire anyway. The badboy act was part of the heat; I knew that better than anyone.

Unfortunately, tonight my cock had a different idea.

The second he got a lubed finger into my asshole, I got hard again. This wouldn't normally be a problem, but the odd thing was that I was getting into the idea of being fucked. I usually preferred to let my mind drift while it went on, keeping my sphincter relaxed and letting the get it over with, but tonight some wanting-to-be-mounted urge was getting the better of me in embarrassing ways, and it was all I could do to keep myself from squirming against his hand. He took a long, careful time lubing me—in his inexperience he seemed really worried about hurting me—and by the time he got two fingers in and touched my prostate, it was starting to get frustrating. I growled in spite of myself and thrust backward.

"You really want this, don't you?" he teased. "All that cold contractual stuff, and underneath you really just want this." *Shut up, damn you, and fuck me! It's embarrassing enough as it is.* "Tell me what you want," he ordered.

Bullshit. I was not going to play this game. "Is this about what I want, or what you want?" I grated out.

"You know what I want," he said.

"Then do it!" He kept messing around with his fingers, as if he hadn't heard. I reached down and took hold of my cock; it was rock-hard. What was worse was that my fangs were unsheathing themselves. I bit at the pillow in annoyance and wanting. All right, fine. After as many years as I'd had in this business, you'd think I wouldn't have any pride left. *It's just a trick,* I told myself. *It doesn't matter. You can say anything you want, as long as you get paid. You'll probably never see him again.* "Fuck me," I said between clenched teeth.

"What?"

"Fuck me, dammit!" I yelled, and, thank the gods, he didn't say another word. I felt his thighs line up against mine, and then the head of his cock slid into my sphincter, which hardly objected at all. I pressed myself back until he was in me to the hilt, and proceeded to beat off onto the bedsheets. He fucked me for a fairly long time considering I'd had him pegged as the fast-coming time, and then came while pressing his face into the leather on my back. I could hear him sniffing it, rubbing against it.

We pulled apart and lay on our backs, him still making moaning noises and "Oh God," and me staring at the ceiling. *Thanks a lot,* I told my asshole. *I really needed you to do that to me with a trick, and a first-time trick at that.* I felt his hand on my arm, stroking me. "You're so good," he said. "You're so good."

Yeah, I'm a professional, dude. Some residual annoyance with myself made me look him in the eye and say, "I started sucking cock for money at the age of fourteen." He blinked and looked away for a moment, and I sighed. That hadn't been exactly fair. My choices were my own, and he did seem to be impressed.

The guy—I still didn't know his name—buried his face in the sleeve of my jacket. "I have this feeling of wanting to keep you here," he said quietly.

Every muscle in my body froze into steel. Was this a psycho? I found myself remembering the bars at the window, wondering if I could break through them and get to the street below. It would hardly be the first trick I'd climbed down three stories to escape. He raised his head and must have seen the expression on my face, because he rushed to reassure me. "Oh, no, no, I didn't mean—I just want to see you again, that's all! I know I couldn't really keep—I mean. . . ." He trailed off, looking worried, and I relaxed.

"It's OK," I said. "I'm around. We can make another appointment." I looked at him. "So why haven't you been with another guy since high school?"

He flushed a little. "I've just been putting things off. Like my life." Now it was his turn to stare at the ceiling. "I was afraid of making it official."

"So is it?"

"What?" He came out of his reverie and blinked at me.

I grinned at him. "Are you a fag yet?"

"Almost," he whispered. His hand moved mine to his bare ass cheeks.

"I can fix that too," I said. "No problem." He wasn't bad, I thought, in spite of all his little digs at me when I was ass in the air. Not as bad as some. And he did have a nice butt, when it was up and ready for me to fuck. I took as long a time to lube him as he had me, but considering how much bigger my cock was, it was probably a good thing. He groaned the same when my cockhead passed his sphincter as he had when my mouth went down on him. I'll forgive a lot in a trick when I've got them under me, especially if they cuss and yell for more while I'm slamming them back and forth on my dick. Especially if they want it even more than I do.

"God, I needed that," he moaned, lying flat on the bed afterward. I chuckled and turned him over, nipped at his arm and chest, let him see my fangs. I was playing fast and loose with my usual scenario of nonthreatening hustler; any moment now he could get scared and book, and I'd have to let him. It was easier and safer to play harmless and pliable until my teeth were in a trick's neck. He didn't run, though; just stared in fascination as his tongue quickly moistened his lips. "Time to pay, huh?" he asked.

"Yep," I said, and forced his head to the side. Gently, but I let him see how strong I really was. Then I dove for his carotid.

There's no way to explain what feeding is like. I've done crack, back before, and I don't give a damn that it doesn't have any effect on me now because feeding is better. Some of us go impotent after the change, and although I didn't I wouldn't care that much if I had, because feeding is better. It's not an activity where you moan and writhe. Once I start sucking, I'm caught in a dead silent fixation of ecstasy, suspended in time, with only the trained reflex of my Black Sun mantras to keep me from draining someone in a mindless haze. One mantra, two, three, and I'm up off him, gasping like I've come up out of deep water. I'm not the only one who's described it that way.

I paused and calmed myself with deep breaths, the colors dancing behind my eyelids. Everything was suddenly very bright, very loud, very sharp. My trick was looking at me with That Look, the awed eyes of the recently fed on. I realized it was probably time to go. "I've got to shoot," I said, preparing to wrench myself to my feet. "Got to get out before the buses stop."

"Stay." His hand was on my arm. "The room's paid through the day. Or you could come home with me," he suggested.

Oh, right. "You sure that's a good idea?" I asked, glancing at him through narrowed eyes. It's not always smart to be around when they come down and realize it was all just another drug in its own way.

He paused and seemed to check himself. "All right," he said. "Stay here tonight. If I still think it's a good idea tomorrow, you can move in with me."

Now it was turn to blink. The first part of that statement made sense, but . . . "I'm not some boy to do your dishes and laundry, man."

"Do whatever you want. You can come and go, whatever, just. . . ." He trailed off as I deliberately let a thin trickle of spit, stained with his blood, trail down my chin, and then quickly licked it back up again. Remind him what he was laying in bed with. He was giving me the fascinated look again—or was it a scientist's look, someone who wanted me under a microscope? I had him pegged as a nerd, maybe an engineer? It didn't matter; his cock was hard again against my thigh. Liked that little display of theatrics, did you? My not-very-small ego gave a warm purr and I rolled over on my stomach, letting him see my bare ass again. It's good to feel desired, even by tricks, when you're a monster.

He ran a hand over my ass, slipped a finger between my cheeks, and before I know it I was hard again too, and my hole was twitching with that annoying urge. *What is up with you tonight*, I asked my nether region silently. Acting like a fuck-starved bitch in heat, as if we didn't get all the sex we wanted any day of the week. I glanced over at his little cock, which was rubbing itself against my leg. Just the right size, didn't hurt a lick going in. Oh well, if one has the urge, one should give it what it wants and shut it up when it's possible. And he did say the room was paid for.

"Want to do it again?" I asked, turning on my side so that his dickhead poked itself right up against my still-slippery asshole. I grabbed my cock and squirmed back against him, figuring he wouldn't argue.

He laughed and wrapped his arms around me from behind. "You really hate this job, don't you," he murmured ironically in my ear.

"Shut up," I said as his cock slid into me. Taking his encircling arm in my free hand, I sank my fangs into the delicate blue lines in his pale, slender wrist.

What We Are Meant to Be

Robert Knippenberg

Afterward she lies close in the crook of my arm, her hand on my chest, her fingers spread in gentleness. Her breasts are warm against my side and I can feel the deep clean thud of her heart slowing as her excitement ebbs. I lightly stroke her face, pushing back the dark wetted curls from her precious temples with my fingertips. I do it to tease myself, gauging my hunger.

She mistakes my gesture, thinking it only the expression of the tenderness I feel for her. She kisses my chest and presses her damply satisfied pussy ardently against the angle of my hip. I can feel the pulse of her youthful vibrancy in the sweetly puffy lips of her vulva.

"That was unbelievable," she murmurs, and even in those three words I can hear the lilt of her Castilian accent, the soft stirring sound that had first led me to notice her among all the others.

I always ensure that it is "unbelievable," or "fantastic," or "wonderful" for them. It is the least that I can do.

"Will you stay the night?" she says, her lips and tongue tickling my skin.

She looks up at me, her eyes hopeful black marbles, glinting beneath half open lids.

"If you want me to," I say.

She mistakes the huskiness in my voice for the desire she wants to hear.

"I want. I want to snuggle and rest for a few moments. But then I want to do it again. If I fall asleep, I want you to fuck me anyway, as soon as you are ready. I want the feel of you slowly sliding inside to awaken me." She grins shyly at me. I can tell that she is surprised and a little shocked by the things she hears herself saying, that she is, at the same time, happy that she can say them to me.

My heart goes out to her then, as it had not before. Of course, she did not have to tell me aloud what she wanted. I know she wants this, even as I knew when we began, although she had been too shy to ask me then, that she wanted me to arouse her with my tongue. I always know what they want, even when they do not know they want it. It is part of what I am. Sometimes when it is especially good, as it has been with her, it is all that I am.

And as I have done uncounted times, although not always inevitably, I wish it could be different, that there was some other way. Especially when they're so youthful and inexperienced as she, when they are as hesitant at first as she had been. And then, once we began, so trusting, so vulnerable. And finally, so frankly passionate.

Her large dark eyes begin to flutter helplessly as she slips into that state of perfect quiet, the happy peace that follows complete sexual gratification. The "petit mort"

the French call it. Although when I am in a woman's or a man's bed, it is a sleep which is anything but small and unimportant. This is the time I prefer to take them, although it was not always so.

In the beginning, I preferred the moment of climax, sating myself at the very instant when their hearts beat most wildly. I was crueler then, but I could not help it. I was what I was, as I am now what I have become.

For most, the question of what I am would largely be answered by my gender. I am, most of the time and at this moment, a man.

And while it's true that I have always found a certain level of comfort with being a male and consider it more or less my normal physical as well as psychological state, since that was what I was in the beginning, this most basic determiner of character is not a valid indicator of the true nature of my being.

"Who are you really?" she asks sleepily.

Her question surprises me. She had not doubted me when I introduced myself as the ship's navigator. And despite her modesty, her reticence, in the ensuing hours in which we'd danced and talked and laughed, it had been easy to make her feel completely at ease with me.

Of course I had by then already become completely the man she wanted me to be. I had let the transformation begin earlier in the evening, while she was still on stage, entertaining the ship's company with the songs of her native Spain. There was something about the way her delicate fingers plucked the strings of her guitar, the way her soft voice first silenced then filled the room. Whatever our gender, whatever our motives, we are all naturally drawn to youth, to beauty, to innocence. But these are not my sole criteria. Beneath her vulnerability I sensed a vitality, a hopefulness. I'd sat down, as helpless as an empty cup—Ah, that first splash, that winey flavor of romantic dreams! She'd filled me up, and I began to change, to allow the heady flavor of her sinless, physical desires to quench for at least a moment the hollowness which is always inside me.

In the few hours we had so far shared we had already been more intimate than some are in a lifetime. But this had not prepared me to expect her question. However, in the wondrous semiconscious dream state that follows a consuming act of love, sometimes the more perceptive will discern that I am not what I appear to be. Such insights are genuinely rare, but when you have lived for as long as I have, almost nothing is new. I have been asked before and it always pleases me.

"It's very difficult to say," I reply, knowing she will not remember my words, but hoping as I had not dared to hope in a long time, that just for once, if I were to let her live beyond the night, she might remember.

Many times before I had optimistically allowed it in certain cases. I was still experimenting then, still desperately unwilling to accept my uniqueness. But always, meeting my lover of the previous night, by chance as far as they knew, I was inevitably disappointed. I found their minds once again clouded over with doubts, the moment of clarity they had displayed during our joyful union gone completely, just as the night had been banished by the morning's light. And then, more sadly than they knew, I would sweep them into bed again, seducing them so swiftly this time they would find themselves confused at being so suddenly naked and overwhelmed by their lust. And I would not hesitate the second time to end, for all eternity, all their doubts, all their confusions.

"I really have no name. I have lived for so long that I have almost forgotten who or what I was in the beginning.

Whoever I am, you will never again meet anyone like me. I know I never have," I say jokingly.

We had talked like this for much of the evening, pretending to be characters from different times and places. She seemed to enjoy it immensely, saying and doing things her natural reticence would not have normally allowed.

It began when we were discussing her songs. She had written some of them herself, remarking that they were based on old stories that her grandmother had told her as a child and when she sang them she often felt as if she were living the lives her lyrics evoked. I too had said that my mother had often read such tales to me as a child and that I had often spent hours acting out the roles of the various heroes and villains as I grew older.

Of course, I said this because I was responding to her romantic nature. Actually my mother had been illiterate, but since the essence of my life is being the consummate actor (or actress, depending on the sexual role my chosen partner prefers) it was actually closer to the truth about myself than anything I could have made up.

Perhaps it was this, or because of something else about her, some emotion in her that uncharacteristically I could not identify, that I began flirting with the idea of being more candid with her than I can ever remember wanting to be with anyone before.

"Well, start at the beginning then," she says, hugging me and wiggling her pretty toes to tickle the sole of my foot. Her eyes are closed tightly now. She seems suddenly less the wanton young woman, more the small child, her cuddling more like a child's sensuality, her sexuality more a yearning for the reassuring comfort of a larger physical presence, her desire more the simple need to be cradled in a parent's arms.

She is just beginning her life and I know from my experience that the beginnings of things are the hardest part of all. I wonder how to begin my story, how to tell her how I began when I do not even believe it myself anymore. Especially since, given my beginnings and all the years and all the lovers, I have come to realize that most of what people take for granted as real is almost entirely superficial. Besides, exactly how I was created is still as mysterious to me as the question of how, if ever, I will end.

"Very well," I say, forcing down my urge to feed, but doing it now to indulge myself. For the moment I am satisfied to feast on her only with my eyes, to drink in the delicious sight of her naked, perfectly proportioned, diminutive body wrapped sweetly around me. I savor the way her hips flare up graciously from her small waist, the slightly shadowed cunning hollow of her buttock, the way her thighs taper down like arrows pointing to her dimpled knee. Then, swelling and slimming again, her leg narrows to the consummate crystal stem of her ankle before blossoming into the shy and dainty flower of her petal perfect foot.

"But I must warn you, some of it will sound fantastic. Although I shall endeavor to tell you the truth, when one lives as I have lived, one is in danger of becoming a myth even to one's self."

I long to warn her further, to tell her that even over the space of a single life span, the human memory is tenuous at best and she must capture every second of every moment, for any one can be her last, or if not, can be a time which she may one day wish she could relive. And even as I long to go on, suddenly wanting to give her advice as a father would his daughter, I am aware that the ache of my hunger is growing and it is this, as much as knowing she has so few moments left, that stops me.

Again what I say to her, I say lightly, not wanting to alarm her. Little does she know that many of my little jokes tonight have been entirely serious, that what I have just told her is another truth which I have told only to a very few before and which none have ever dared to comprehend.

"Ah, you are not just a character! You are a living myth! That explains it. That must be why I find you so utterly enchanting," she says with a sighing giggle.

Her soft little laugh would have been inaudible to anyone with normal hearing. All my senses are, however, anything but normal. Not only can I hear her clearly, but I feel as well the tiny tremors of her body against my side, and hear as well as feel the slight increase in the rhythm of her heart.

All this fans the heat of my dual desires. Everything she says and does, each tiny sound, each little movement, only makes my hunger for her life force grow, thereby adding to her danger. At the same time, these same things make my cock stir and augment my desire to make love to her once more and thereby she prolongs her existence by just that much. Such conflict is rare and I find it delightful.

"It sounds very much as if I am in for a very long story. The story of your life perhaps?" she asks.

"Perhaps, but what is any life if not a story? The question is not whether it is a story, or even if it is a true story, or even how long it is. The question is whether or not it is an interesting story."

"I love long stories. As long as they are interesting," she says, giggling again, this time at her own remark.

"Once upon a time, there lived in a new and faraway land, a bright young boy full of hope, full of promise."

"Once upon a time?" she says, grinning and stifling a yawn at the same moment. "Once upon a time?"

"All the best stories begin that way."

I have been lightly caressing the smoothness of her back as we talk. Now I reach around to cup her breast as I stretch my neck to kiss her forehead. It is what she needs, these little reassurances. I can feel these things even when others are not aware they want them. Such feelings are the essence of my talent for seduction.

She moans a little, hugs me back with her body.

"I thought you were going to sleep?" I say.

"Yes, I'm sorry but I need to. Just for a few moments. I have had so little sleep for the last week, worrying about this trip. It is the first time I have ever been on ocean liner. But only if you promise to wake me up as I asked."

"I promise," I say and suddenly I know I can keep my promise. This exceptional girl has charmed me so that I find a renewed strength in myself and it is easier to hold back my hunger than I had ever thought possible.

"Then tell me your story. And I promise I shall hear it even if I am asleep."

And so I begin again.

Once upon a time—I forget the exact year, but it was in the 1670s—there was a boy in the town of Salem in the Colony of Massachusetts. His mother and father were more religious than most in the community and he was much affected, because of their grim fervor, by serious thoughts. He spent hours contemplating good and evil and wondering about the angels and devils and witches he heard the minister speak about each Sunday in church.

He was a handsome boy, and by the age of fourteen he had already almost attained the physical size and strength of a grown man. But in his heart he was troubled. His developing sexuality battled with the principles his parents and his teachers had ingrained in him so deeply and he felt at war within himself. He often had spontaneous erections in school and in church, and at night he found himself dreaming of the girls he knew—and sometimes even their mothers—undressing for him and revealing what they looked like underneath their layers of severe clothes. He dared not talk of this to anyone; to escape his sinful urges, he would often spend hours wandering in the woods, mentally scourging himself and praying to God to be released from them.

To escape his anguish, he began to watch the forest animals, wishing he had been born as simple and as innocent as God made them. Soon he became skilled at stalking and spying on them. But the more he watched them, the more he realized that they were not at all the uncomplicated creatures he had supposed. Their behaviors and the dramas of their lives seemed to echo back to him the very conflicting emotions he had come to the woods to forget.

He was shocked but at the same time excited by the promiscuity of the nesting songbirds and the frenzied orgies of the rabbits. He was sickened but also thrilled by the rapacity of the cunning vixen fox, killing and ripping apart her prey. He was repelled and yet haunted by the cool evil slyness of the snake, silently robbing the nests of the licentious birds, devouring fledglings or swallowing whole eggs with his unhinged jaws.

But most of all he was affected by the haughty spiraling of the hunting hawks. He would watch them for hours—listening to their cries, which never failed to send chills throughout his body, pretending he was with them, high above the earth, free from doubt and sin. And then one day one seemed to be calling him. He closed his eyes and suddenly he saw the world below, small and clear and perfect in each detail. Then he felt the hawk's hunger and, when the bird stooped, he felt the wind in his face, heard the screaming of the air past his ears. And then, the tiny final, infantile cry and the hot gush of blood through soft fur as he speared the rabbit with his magnificently taloned feet made him sob aloud with a terrible joy. . . .

The first time this happened he was horrified, sure it was only further evidence of his evil nature. But he could not stop and he flew with the hawk again. Then he found he could run with the fox and crawl with the snake as well. He realized now that unlike what everyone believed, the animals lived rich and vital lives. And further, that their vivid feelings and emotions, so real and so like his, were more powerful and real than what he had been taught human emotions were supposed to be. Now he began to question everything he had been taught, and this troubled him even more.

He tried to talk to his father about this, asking him about God's reasons for the creation of the animals and why they were the way they were, but his stern and pious father told him only to go read his Bible, where all the answers to all questions were vouchsafed to the faithful.

Earnestly he re-read Genesis again and again. And then, determinedly, but now losing any real hope, he studied the other books of both the Old and New Testaments. But as he feared, they held no answers to the questions raised by the things he had seen and experienced. He felt more alone then ever in his struggle with the conflicting urges he felt growing inside him. In his shame and doubt he began spending less and less time with his friends and family and more and more time alone.

And so it was that one day he wandered further into the forest than he ever had before, where he chanced upon a little well-kept cottage all by itself in a clearing in the woods. There he saw a woman working in her garden. He observed her secretly, using the stealth he had taught himself while watching the animals. It was very strange for anyone to be living so far away from the settlement, and the only reason he could imagine that anyone would do so was that she was one of the witches that the minister had warned everyone against.

And as he had been drawn to the behavior of the animals, he went back whenever he could, sure that he would eventually catch her performing some evil or unnatural act. Usually she was outside, but sometimes he spied on her through her windows from the branches of the trees. But always the pretty cottage was the picture of everyday goodness and she would be gardening, or spinning, or tending her little flocks of chickens and geese, or carrying out some other ordinary household task.

But the boy could not accept that everything was as it appeared. Not only did she live by herself and seem to be prospering, a thing unusual enough in itself, but no matter what she was doing or how long he watched, she always seemed to sit or stand or move in such a way that her large starched bonnet inevitably obscured her face. Furthermore, no matter what she was doing, she moved with an uncommonly easy grace, almost as if she were naked like the animals instead of being hampered by the thick layers of dark clothes that she and all women wore to disguise their femininity.

He became obsessed by her and by his musings on her true nature. And so he returned, again and again, becoming increasingly frustrated by his inability to see her face or discover anything else unnatural about her and growing more bold and less careful each time.

Finally, unable to bear it any longer, he walked up to her one day as she was hoeing. She had her back to him and he had made no sound as he approached. He was a well-mannered boy and had been taught to wait until an adult addressed him before he spoke. Furthermore he was afraid to speak for fear of startling her, so he stood, wondering what to do, watching the way her back and shoulders moved as she chopped away with her hoe between the rows of lush vegetables and blooming fragrant flowers. Then he noticed that there were no little weeds trying to gain a foothold where she was working, nor for that matter anywhere in her garden, and everywhere the rich dark earth was already loose and fluffy.

"It took you long enough," she said and he could hear her amusement like music in her voice.

She moved to the next row, her back still to him. The boy knew that not only was she aware of him, but that she had always known when he was there.

But this did not surprise him half as much as the sudden realization that he had always known that she knew.

"Who are you?" he said.

"That is difficult to say," she said, stopping finally. She let her hoe drop and she turned to face him. Then she untied and removed her bonnet.

"Who would you like me to be?"

To say that she was incredibly beautiful would be to mislead you. She was, but that was only a small part of what she was.

The boy was stunned by her, for her hair was the same vibrant color as the fox when it ran in the sunlight, and her eyes were flecked with gold like the hawk's and had their piercing brilliancy that saw everything, and her gaze was coolly hypnotic like the snake, and her skin was as clear and smooth as the whitest unblemished bird's egg, and her voice was as enchanting as the most melodious song a bird had ever sung.

And so the boy stood frozen, not knowing what her question meant, but unable to move or even to speak to ask her.

"Come inside," she said smiling. She took his hand and he was released, sure that before that moment he had never seen a smile, had never felt another's fingers.

He followed her as the faithful dog follows his master. Inside he saw what he was always sure was there but had never been able to see from his perch in the faraway tree. The walls of the cottage were lined with shelves of glass jars, earthen urns, little wooden boxes, and small colored stones that seemed to glow with their own internal light. And, their whiteness bright in the dimness, he saw the bones and skulls of small animals and the large white mushrooms that grew on the trunks of rotting trees, and other things he could not readily identify from their shape and color.

Staring around him he managed at last to speak. "You are a witch!" he gasped.

"You may call me that if it pleases you, and I can tell that it does. But why, if I am what you think, are you not afraid?"

She was right, but the boy had no answer.

"You think that witches are old and ugly, but you find me attractive instead. Is that it?"

"Yes. Yes that's true. But how do you know?"

"I know what is important to know about others. I know how they feel."

Then she went to the large wooden bathing tub in one corner and dragged it across the floor in front of the hearth. She picked up two wooden buckets and holding one out to him said, "I even know their most secret dreams. . . ."

And feeling as if he were dreaming, he followed her outside to the well where they filled the buckets, and then back inside to pour the fresh cool water into the tub.

Then, as she poured steaming water into the tub from the large kettle that hung above the fire, she said, "You may take off your clothes now. It's time for your bath."

He began by removing his boots, feeling as natural as if he were at home. But there his mother would leave the room as soon as he did this. It had been so ever since he became old enough to bathe on his own.

For that matter, neither his mother nor his father touched him or even each other at all except when necessary. They believed that the body was only a temporary housing for the soul and that the devil used a person's body to tempt the soul to forget itself, to distract the heart from the path of purity that God had intended.

But she was testing the water, stirring it with her hand, and as he removed the last of his clothes he knew she was not going to leave. Then, his blood pulsing, his breathing quickened, he became aware of his sinful, rising flesh.

Ever since he could remember he had loved his bath. And ever since he could remember he had been unable to resist the sin of playing with himself beneath the soapy water. He would start out vowing not to, pretending it was his mother's hands that were washing him slowly and carefully everywhere else.

But eventually his hand, almost by itself, would slip down and he would already be hard with anticipation. He would begin with the briefest of touches, until at the end, arching his hips up, he would close his eyes, imagining that it was his mother's fingers gripping and tugging on him, that she was forcing the evil fluid to spurt out of him, splash hotly on his belly.

Afterward, he would open his eyes, watch the evidence of his sin float away in small disappearing spirals as he let his hips sink slowly beneath the water. And then, alone in the terrible peace that always followed this inevitable act of release, he would pretend his mother was kneeling next to the tub, hugging him and kissing his cheeks and telling him how much she loved him.

"For a handsome young boy, you are already quite a man," the woman said. She was smiling, looking frankly at his cock. Her eyes and lips made him aware that it was filling, growing. This made his face turn even redder. He stepped quickly into the tub and sat down, but it was a blush of pride and happiness and not shame her words and grin made him feel.

She soaped a cloth and began to wash him. Her touch seemed to excite and at the same time soothe both his mind and body.

Now he relaxed even more as he laid back against the comfortably carved contour of the wooden bath. Her hands felt as natural as the rain as they moved slowly over his neck and shoulders and chest. He closed his eyes, felt the love he had always yearned for in her caress. She washed his legs next and he felt like an infant again as she purred over his toes, kissing them and then the soles of his feet, then his knees.

She told him stand so she could wash the rest of him. Her hands on his ass and balls and cock made him tingle with a lingering intensity all out of proportion to the innocence of her brief touches.

She finished washing him and took his hand, had him step out of the tub. Then, looking at him, and all the while smiling, she undressed before him and she was the perfect physical fulfillment of his dreams.

The boy felt no guilt or shame that the sight of her perfect body made his cock completely rigid. Instead it was as if all his depraved imaginings, all his impure thoughts, were suddenly wholesome and upright. He felt happy and complete being naked in front of her and his cock became the most honest part of his body.

She began to dry him with a soft towel and again he closed his eyes. Then the towel was gone and it was just her hands caressing him gently and intimately. He could feel her warmth as she stood close, her presence such that any moment he was sure the space between them would vanish, that they would become one being, and the thought that such a thing might be possible excited him even more.

Then he felt the warmth of her breath on his face as she kissed him. Her lips moved thrillingly over his neck and shoulders. Her tongue briefly tickled the nipples of his breasts, then moved slowly downward, delighting his belly.

He opened his eyes then, looked down to see her kneeling before him. He saw her close her eyes as she put her hands on his hips and leaned to put her lips on the tip of his cock. She kissed it lovingly for a moment, just as she had his toes, then took it into her mouth. It was as astonishing an act as he had ever seen, something he had never even thought of imagining.

Then she began sucking on him and it was a more marvelous sensation than he had ever imagined. It made him feel helpless and more powerful than he had ever been, and flames of lust flared up from his loins to consume his useless soul. He closed his eyes again, already feeling the need to ejaculate. She gripped him harder now, holding him steady as she took all of him deeper into her mouth. Then, as the head of his cock touched the back of her throat, he began. He could feel as well as hear her swallowing, as if she needed every drop, as if his semen were an elixir she had to have to sustain her life. He could no longer tell the difference between his body and her mouth, between his soul and hers, between good and evil, or God and the Devil, or Heaven and Hell. Everything seemed suddenly to be one and the same thing and he wanted to embrace it all and fling himself into the oneness, the emptiness, to fill it up.

The spasms went on and on, his balls pumping wildly, forcing his burning fluid through the tube of his cock as if he contained the sins of the world and they would flow from him forever—then he knew she was eating him! Not with her mouth and not his flesh, but *him*—his essence, his life force.

He desperately pulled away. As soon as they were no longer touching he saw, flickering in front of him, a thing so hideous and old as to be almost sexless and inhuman. He knew then that everything he had thought she was had been only an illusion.

Her breathing is gentle and deep and this time her soft hand is limp upon my chest. She had fallen asleep long ago and despite her promise, could not have heard my story.

I decide to take her now, to suck her life essence into me, as that creature had tried to do to me so long ago.

Gently, I disentangle myself from her, moving slowly and carefully so I do not disturb her. I lay next to her, to place my mouth on her lips, but then she sighs and rolls over on her back, her small hands open with her palms up and her legs open like a child's. I look down at her, so vulnerable in her sleep and again the twin desires surge, warring within me. If only she had not moved. If only she did not look so enchantingly available.

But she does, and as I look at her I decide there is time yet. I have forever. I can give her a few moments more. Instead I decide to first fulfill my promise to her. It is the least that I can do. Besides, my cock has grown hard and pulses with the sight of her, and this makes my decision easier.

I position my knees between hers, using them to carefully push hers apart.

Then, holding myself up on one arm, I gently work the head of my cock against the pretty lips that guard her precious opening, easing myself in further. Her lovely cunt is warm and still wet. Using both arms now to hold myself above her so our bodies do not touch anywhere else, I move with gentle thrusts until I am in all the way. The way her rippled walls lovingly envelop me makes me tremble and her almost-virginal tightness makes my cock twitch. Then I begin, moving ever so slightly, just as she had wanted. Her breathing changes as her insides respond, welcoming me.

Moments later she moans in her sleep. I have been teasing her, knowing that she loves being smothered under the body of her lover. Now I dip my head to tickle her erect nipples with my tongue. She wraps her arms around me to pull me down on top of her, whimpering as she thrusts her hips up to meet mine.

It took me almost all of the first hundred years of my existence to discover how to gain complete control over my physical body. Now I use my skill at changing shape and she gasps with delight as my cock swells to fit her shape inside exactly. This time I stretch her a bit more and she begins to murmur, small Spanish words that tell me she has never before been filled so wonderfully, so completely.

This time her mood is not one of gentle romance, as it had been when I first seduced her. I respond to her unconscious wishes, putting her arms up over her head, imprisoning her wrists with my hands. I peg her legs apart with my feet and begin to plunge into her, ramming my pelvis hard against her until her body shudders.

This feeds and fulfills her fantasies of being taken against her will. Her trilled, Castilian endearments become a thrilling babble of sweet and wild obscenities, punctuated by the groans she makes each time I penetrate her deeply and stop, make my cock writhe as if it were something alive inside her. Soon she has abandoned the last shred of her inhibitions. She begs me loudly, and in English, to fuck her harder and faster and just like this forever.

At moments like this it is always been as if I am two beings in the same shell—one participating fully in the sexual madness of the moment, feeling a genuine passion, the other aloof, determining my partner's moods and needs and coolly analyzing my own. And now with her heart beating so hard and wildly against me, I can barely contain either of my selves. One moment I love her, the next I want to take her life.

I feel her orgasm building swiftly deep inside her. I ready myself and when it bursts upon her, I know her life force is at its fullest flower. My hunger too is peaking, but once again, something about her holds me back, some quality that I cannot yet identify. Instead of taking her, I flood her with my come, submerging my hunger in the joy she is giving me, in the rapture I am giving her.

Finally her shuddering slows and stops. Sensing the change in her need, I roll away, freeing her to breathe, so she can begin her return to the sad and terrible state that all ordinary human beings take to be reality.

I light cigarettes for us both and we hold hands as we smoke. She turns on the light on her side of the bed, wanting to see the smoke curling up. It is late and has been dark for a long time, but since I can see as well in the dark as others see in the light, I never bother with the lights.

Looking at her, the flush of her cheeks, the softness of her eyes, the lush slackness of her lips, I want to kiss her, but I do not dare.

"Thank you for keeping your promise," she says, squeezing my hand. "It was even better than I hoped it would be."

"And did you keep yours?" I reply, smirking, raising a brow.

"Of course. So what did the boy do after he discovered the beautiful woman was really a witch?"

Now I look even more closely at her. "You heard me even though you were asleep?"

"Not heard exactly. I don't remember your voice after a certain point, but I remember the pictures your words created. Like a movie in my head."

"That is quite a remarkable talent," I say, wondering—because she is grinning back at me like a smug and beautiful cat—what else there is about her that I have yet to learn. And perhaps, just perhaps, if she has something else to teach me.

"I have been able to do it ever since I was a little girl. I so wanted to hear the stories my grandmother was reading to me, so even though I went to sleep, I heard them. And then later I would see them and let them play over and over again in my head. It made me a rather poor student in school, I'm afraid."

"But it gave you a rich imagination. That is far more important than the things they teach in school."

"Perhaps, but an imagination does not help you make a living. Except in the arts. That is why I took up singing and writing songs."

"You have a haunting voice. And your songs are wise beyond your years. And now I find that you make love as beautifully as you sing about it. Such a wondrously candid sexuality is remarkable in anyone, and especially in one so young. Is this too a product of your imagination, or have you had that many lovers?"

"Not so many," she says, sitting up to put out her cigarette. "But they don't count in any case." She snuggles close to me again and is silent for a moment. And then, and her face is against my arm so that I also feel her lips form the words, "You are my first real lover. And you shall never leave me," she whispers.

Her words both warm and chill me. I know I am not the first man she has ever slept with, but neither is what she says a lie. And now I begin to enjoy this odd way she has of making me feel a little unsure of myself, as if everything she's said and done was a threat as well as an entreaty.

And this ambivalence I have been feeling from the beginning takes on a new and deeper meaning, becomes doubly odd, since I know I have nothing to fear from her. Long ago I tried more than once to end my life, but poisons, bullets, fire, water, even leaping from a tall building, never accomplished anything but a temporary agony. I suspect an explosion that would destroy my body completely might work, but I cannot stand the idea that it might not, that I would only experience a much longer and more terrible torture only to find myself whole again and everything the same.

But even though I welcome this unique and unfamiliar mix of foreboding and delight and would love to spend a few more hours with her to find out what it is that makes her so different from all the others, my hunger is making this impossible. It is time to end this, and to this end I reach over her, as if I were merely putting out the light. Then, pretending I am so distracted by her that I have to kiss her instead, I lean down to cover her mouth with mine for the last time.

But she laughs and squirms away. Then her mouth on my cock distracts me from my purpose. She stops after a few moments and crawls back up beside me, lifting my arm and placing it around her so she can nestle beneath it again.

"Is that what I taste like?" she says. Her lips glisten now even more prettily from the combined liquids of our love.

"Yes. Your exquisite little pussy is quite delicious. You've never tasted yourself before?"

"No. There are many things I've never done before. I've never asked a man to spend the night. And I've never put a man's cock in my mouth. I never wanted to until I heard your story."

This much at least was true. "And did you like it?"

"Your cock in my mouth or your story?" she teases.

I have to laugh. "Either one!"

"I liked them both. But the one is not ready to begin again and the other has not ended."

"Would you like to hear the rest of the story while my cock rests until it's ready to give you pleasure again?"

"I will not let you go until you do."

"Do which?"

"Both."

We both laugh and kiss. It is strangely easy to kiss her now and our two tongues share the flavors of both our sexes. Then I light another cigarette and she settles back. I begin again, once more feeling like the father cuddling his sweet young daughter, ready to tell her a fairy tale.

The boy dashed out of the cottage, running as fast as he could through the woods and meadows. He did not dare to look back, but he listened for her footsteps, kept glancing down at his own bare pounding feet, for now he knew the terror of the rabbit and was sure that at any moment he'd see her shadow, that he'd be taken, that her darkness that would descend on him like the final shadow of the hawk's looming wings.

He was so terrified he forgot he was naked until he saw the horrified faces of the people in the street. And when they gathered around him all he had the breath left to say was, "A witch, a witch!" as he collapsed in their arms.

For two days he stayed in bed, seemingly delirious with fever. His body was hot and his face was flushed, but the boy knew this was no ordinary sickness. What had begun as a maddeningly delicious tingling in his now perpetually rigid cock was spreading up his belly and down his legs and the boy believed his sin was still with him, that it was changing him slowly. In penance, he refused all food and drink and prayed incessantly to God to make the feeling stop. Finally his mother became so distraught she actually tried to hold and comfort him. But this made the tingling even more marvelous and his cock throbbed furiously with a life of its own. "Leave me alone! It's too late!" he screamed, sure this was God's way of punishing him.

Terrified and convinced the boy was under a spell, his mother ran to fetch the minister. Grimly standing over him, huge and certain as a tree—for he had seen, he was sure, such cases before—he insisted the boy tell him who the witch was and where she could be found. The boy resisted, questioning now what he had seen in those few seconds before he ran, certain it had all been the evil inside himself, a fantastic dream for which he alone was responsible.

Finally, when the angry minister threatened him with eternal damnation, he broke down and in exchange for the man's blessing he described the woman as he had first seen her and told him where in the woods to find her cottage, sure that they would search and find nothing.

By the morning of the third day the wonderful burning had spread throughout his body. He stopped praying, emptied by the knowledge that God had abandoned him. By that afternoon, the unnatural sensation began to

subside and his hunger and thirst forced him to leave his
bed at last and dress. He ate and drank then and was
feeling almost normal, when, just as he stepped outside
his house, he saw a group of men leading the beautiful red-
haired woman down the street. She was bound with
enough rope to hold three men and had been blindfolded
so she stumbled in the ruts in the road. Then as she was
led past him, she turned her head and smiled at him, even
though she could not possibly have known he was there.

Suddenly the horror of what he had done struck the boy
like the lightning cleaves the tree. He went back inside,
his heart sick, his mind numb. He complained of fatigue
to his mother and returned again to his bed, where this
time he lay burning with a different fire, the fire of his
love for this woman who would be burned at the stake
because of his accusations. In desperation he tried to pray
again, but discovered he no longer believed there was
anyone to pray to, and in that moment gave up the last
shred of his old religion and wept as he had never wept
before.

The next day he skulked through the crowd of
townspeople gathered in the square, listening to their
whisperings. Her trial had been swift and conclusive, as
somehow he knew it would be. Some were saying that she
had denied nothing, but also said nothing in her own
defense. Others said that she had said she could only be
what they thought she was, but had seemed confused
about what a "witch" was supposed to be. Still others
swore that she had admitted to charming the boy, but
claimed she had done it not to harm him, but to save him.

The words they spoke made him realize how little all
these people cared about each other, how little they
understood the nature of good and evil. He hid his face
from them and was silent, hating them almost as much as
he hated himself. He wanted to run away, to live in the

woods forever, or even better, to die there, but he could not leave her. But neither could he look at her until the very end. Then, when he did, he stared in fascination. She was smiling at him through the acrid smoke, the consuming flames, her eyes as bright and golden as they had been on that sunlit afternoon. She did not appear to be in pain. She made no sound at all. Then she seemed to disappear, as if she had turned completely to ashes in an instant. The watching crowd gasped at this event, which they took as proof of the correctness of their judgment, their solution. But it was then the boy realized his mistake, that he knew she had been real, that instead it was he and his mother and father and everyone in the town who was not.

For days afterwards he thought that at any moment he too would vanish. He became thin, vague, as insubstantial as the air, and at the same time wooden like a puppet, his arms and legs and body doing all the things they had ever done, but without caring, without meaning, without a master to pull the strings.

Strangely, everyone in town spoke to him now, as they hadn't before, but to him his fame was ashes in his mouth, reminding him of her, their friendliness convincing him of the truth he had discovered, that everything was an illusion.

He lived like this for many weeks, not surprised that everyone seemed able to forget the incident, to go on with their small and meaningless lives.

Then one Sunday in church as he sat with head bowed, staring at the floor pretending he was praying, he became aware that the young blond boy next to him was looking at him. He looked back, saw that the boy had long dark lashes and large dark pleading eyes.

The boy's fantasy flashed through him then. It was the first time he had ever felt the desire of another, experienced another's hopes and dreams. What the boy wanted was clear and perfect in his mind and, despite its perversity, was exquisite in its guiltlessness. And even more astounding was the fact that it was the first thing, the only thing he felt was real since the day the red-haired woman was burned.

The boy quickly looked away. But as he left the church, he could feel the heat of the boy's body, as though he were naked and carrying him on his back. Startled, he turned to see the boy stop some distance behind him. The hunger sprang to life in him then, the hunger that from then on would be his life. He knew he had been transformed, that he was not himself anymore. Or if he was, he was also something else.

He smiled at the boy and the boy smiled back. He told his parents that he would like to be alone, to walk for awhile to ponder the minister's sermon. They went on ahead and he began to walk again, with the boy following.

Arriving at his father's barn, all it took was a glance and the boy waited outside while he went inside to get the things he needed. The boy followed him again, closer this time, as he took the path into the woods.

After awhile he stopped and turned. Both of them were breathing excitedly now. He told the boy to undress, which the lad did without hesitation. He motioned the boy to come closer, and a hand on his trembling shoulder made the boy kneel. He ran his fingers through the fine blond hair on the bent head before him, tasting the lad's unfamiliar desires, taking them as his, understanding the urgency, if not the why, of the boy's needs.

He opened his trousers, lifted the boy's chin. He stared into his frightened, girlish eyes, soothed him with a touch of his fingers on his cheek. The boy smiled, nervously, hopefully, then leaned toward him. He shivered at the first tentative touch of the boy's warm, rosy lips. His flesh filled, stiffened, becoming something real again as the boy began gratefully to suck him. He felt the boy's twisted love being released, and it made him happy he was able to fulfill at last the boy's wish, a tightly coiled desire so lonely and so yet so compelling that often in despair, the lad had longed for the courage to commit the ultimate sin of suicide.

He stopped him when it was time and pointed to the tree he had picked out.

The boy willingly pressed his face and body against the rough bark while he wound around him the rope he had brought. Then, his blood boiling, taking the boy's excited anticipation as his own, he began using the harness strap he had also taken from the barn.

It was clear in the boy's mind so he knew just how hard and where to strike. He beat him just as the boy's father beat him almost every day, but he did it with love instead of hate, with care instead of anger, with compassion instead of fear, because these were what the boy needed.

Then, when the boy's buttocks were sufficiently warmed and reddened, he worked his hard wet cock against the boy's wrinkled rose. Again he took as his own the boy's yearning, giving it back to him, to first soothe his fear, then to share with his the delightful slow hot sliding. When the young boy's small hard cock began to jerk in release against the tree, he bent the boy's head back and to the side. He kissed the boy's lips tenderly for a moment, just as the boy had imagined. Their mouths became eager, hungry for each other, and just as he began to ejaculate deep into the boy's bowels, he sucked the boy's life inside him.

Afterward, filled with a power he never knew existed, he carried the boy's body easily as he walked deeper into the woods. He could see each leaf on every tree, the vibrant colors of each petal of every flower. The sky was brighter and more vividly blue than it had ever been. Everything around him seemed to vibrate with life, and it was all the same life in different forms and guises. Everything seemed to make sense now, although it was not a sense he could have explained to anyone.

He found the clearing where he had seen the red-haired woman, although the cottage and the garden were not there as he had known they would not be.

He laid the boy down in the sun-warmed grass, watched the bent green blades spring up slowly, one-by-one, as the body faded, disappeared.

Then he walked off deeper and farther into the woods and was never heard from again.

"It's a wonderful story. Sad, but wonderful."

Her eyes are shining. I kiss her forehead. She blinks and the tears run down her cheeks.

"I'm glad you liked it."

"Except they didn't burn witches in America, you know. At least not most of them. They were hanged, or crushed under wooden pallets piled up with stones."

"Yes, I know. But it's much more dramatic to have her disappear in a puff of smoke."

"But otherwise it's true, isn't it."

"Yes. At least I think it is. I suppose some of the other details are made up, but the essence is true. At least I think so. It was so long ago."

"Has it been long enough?"

"Yes."

"You're sure?"

"Yes."

"Then, it's time."

She slips down on the bed and again her mouth takes me in. She sucks me gently, as if she were afraid I would break. Her tenderness and her concern make me grow hard that much more quickly.

"I'm sorry if I'm not doing it right," she says. "I'm just beginning."

"I know. Beginnings are the hardest. Endings are much easier."

"I don't want to hurt you."

"Don't worry, you're doing it just right."

She begins moving her hand on me then, sucking harder. I should have known all along. It was obvious, but it's so seductive believing our own illusions.

She stops, knowing I am close. "Are you ready?" she asks.

"Yes."

She does it quickly then. In moments I feel it begin. It is glorious! An orgasm to end all orgasms. An orgasm that is the beginning of everything, and at last I understand— and with this ultimate gift of purpose she makes me happy at last. She is beginning her new life as I had begun mine, but with purpose, with compassion, with comprehension. She knows that one day she will give all the lives I've taken and all the lives she has yet to take to another, and that they will be passed on to yet another and yet another so that someday one of us will become that which encompasses all lives, the God that all of us were always meant to be.

Afterword

This is the third volume of erotic vampire stories I have edited, and my friends are beginning to wonder whether there isn't something more to my nocturnal work habits than the eccentricities of a creative mind. Let them wonder—that is one activity I encourage wholeheartedly. Let us let our imaginations run wild, wondering just what is going on in the dark. It is that kind of mental activity that leads to this kind of book, a book about the mysteries of sex, a book about fear of the unknown, a book about sinful pleasures and pleasureful sins both real and imaginary.

In real life I am not a vampire, I am an erotic activist. When I stay up late into the night, I am not feeding my carnal hungers (usually), but typing away at essays and stories made to open people's eyes to the erotic world around them. I am producing newsletters and preparing lectures. When I edit, I am nurturing the fantasies of other creative minds, refining them, honing them. We have worked those late hours to bring this book to you, and already we are at work on the fourth volume, *A Taste of Midnight*. And so, until then, I bid you adieu, dear reader. Read well and be well.

Cecilia Tan
October 1997

About the Authors

Pete Abrams makes his living as a freelance illustrator and web-designer. His diverse work encompasses everything from video games graphics to designing business-oriented websites. His creativeness and ability to communicate his ideas through images has been key to his success. You can check out his latest project—a daily comic strip—on the internet at www.sluggy.com.

Deb Atwood marks her debut into publication with "A Moment in Time," a landmark in her life which she hopes heralds many similar times to come! The past year of her life has been an eventful one, including marriage, a new house, and the start of a family. Deb masquerades during the daytime hours as a software developer in central New York State. She is still in a state of wonder that she has found a place to share the erotica she has always enjoyed creating.

Gary Bowen has published over a hundred short stories in anthologies and magazines and is the author of *Diary of a Vampire* (Masquerade Books, 1995), a finalist for the Bram Stoker Award in the category of Best First Novel, and the collection *Man Hungry* (Masquerade, 1996). He can often be recognized at science fiction conventions on the East Coast by his white Stetson hat. He contributes regularly to Circlet Press erotic sf/f anthologies. His work can be found in *Wired Hard, Wired Hard 2, Blood Kiss, Fetish Fantastic, SexMagick 2, S/M Pasts, Genderflex, TechnoSex,* and the chapbook *Queer Destinies.*

Rhomylly B. Forbes lives near Washington, DC, with two gay housemates and several small animals. Previous short stories have appeared in the anthologies *Tomboys! Tales of Dyke Derring-Do, Close Calls: New Lesbian Fiction* and *Queer View Mirror II.* She dedicates this story to Kent and Brian, who always care.

Susan Elizabeth Gray is a matrimonial attorney from Western New York who has a secret life as a writer. She has published her short stories in *Artvoice, Libido, Black Sheets,* and *Shoofly* magazines.

Robert Knippenberg began writing porn, smut, erotica (you choose) because it turned him on. He continues to write it almost exclusively because:
• there isn't enough good porn, smut, erotica around
• much of what is around is depressing and/or demeaning   to women and/or men
• our society needs new, happier mythologies to replace   our insane ones about men, women and sex
• it still turns him on.

Catherine Lundoff is a femme top who lives in Min-neapolis with her girlfriend. Her fiction has been accepted for the forthcoming anthologies *Pillowtalk, 1001 Kisses, Lesbian Short Fiction,* and *Powderhorn Writers Anthology.* "El Tigre" won an award in the 1996 Writers Bloc Fiction Contest, where it was described as "disturbing."

David May was a nice boy from a good family who fell in with the wrong crowd. He attended the University of California at Santa Cruz where he studied Dramatic Literature, specializing in medieval religious theatre. He is the author of S/M-oriented *Madrugada: A Cycle of Erotic Fictions.* His work, both fiction and nonfiction, has appeared in *Drummer, Mach, Honcho, Lambda Book Report, Frontiers, Inches, Advocate Men,* and *Cat Fancy.* His fiction also appears in the anthologies *Queer View Mirror, Rogues of San Francisco, Meltdown!* and *Flesh and the Word 3.* He currently lives in San Francisco with his husband, a dog, and three cats.

A.R. Morlan has had erotica published in *Love In Vein: Stories of Erotic Vampirism* and *Deadly After Dark: The Hot Blood Series.* Both stories were reprinted in *The Year's Best Fantasy 1994.* In addition to erotica, she's had short stories published in *The Magazine of Fantasy & Science Fiction, Full Spectrum IV,* and many other magazines and anthologies. She's the author of two novels, *The Amulet* and *Dark Journey* (Bantam), and currently teaches short fiction for a correspondence school.

Thomas Roche is a San Francisco writer, editor, and performer. His short stories have appeared in such anthologies as *Best American Erotica 1996* and *Best American Erotica 1997* and *The Mammoth Book of Pulp Fiction.* Books he edited, co-edited, or wrote include *Dark Matter, Noirotica, Sons of Darkness, Brothers of the Night,* and *Gargoyles.*

Cecilia Tan founded Circlet Press in 1992 and has since edited over two dozen anthologies of erotic fantasy and science fiction. She also teaches workshops on erotic writing, S/M relationships, and turning erotic fantasy into reality. She is the author of the collection of erotic short stories *Black Feathers: Erotic Dreams* (HarperCollins, 1998), the erotic novel *The Velderet* (Masquerade, 1998), and many essays on sex and fantasy.